Marco's Millions

MARCO'S

WILLIAM SLEATOR

MILLIONS

SCHOLASTIC INC.

New York Toronto London Auckland Sydney
Mexico City New Delhi Hong Kong Buenos Aires

ISBN 0-439-45462-X

12 11 10 9 8 7 6 5 4 3 2   4 5 6 7/0

Printed in the U.S.A.   40

First Scholastic printing, November 2002
Designed by Alan Carr

For Andrew Biggs,

my brilliant and famous best friend,

who lives in my favorite part of the world

Marco's Millions

Marco liked to go places—and he thought about millions a lot. *Millions* didn't mean money to him. *Millions* meant distances—and if you're thinking about distances, *millions* means going very, very far away.

One day when Marco was five and his baby sister, Ruth, was screaming, Marco walked out of the house, down to the corner, and got on a bus. He stayed on the bus for hours, watching with fascination the different neighborhoods they drove through.

At the end of the line, everybody got off, and Marco did too. The bus driver changed the sign on the front, and

Marco got back on, asking the driver if the bus went back the way it came. It did. He got home with no problem.

He told his mother he had been playing hide-and-seek with kids in the neighborhood. She believed him. But his four-year-old sister, Lilly, gave Marco a long look. Lilly had a way of knowing things without being told. She always knew what Ruth wanted, even though Ruth couldn't talk. Once, when their father was late coming home from work and their mother was worried because she couldn't reach him, Lilly said he was just having car trouble—and that's what it turned out to be. Now Marco felt she knew where he had been. But he trusted her not to tell their parents. Marco and Lilly were friendly, though Lilly was very shy.

After that, he rode the bus whenever he could scrape the money together, always checking first to make sure no one at home saw where he was going. He took different buses with different routes. He knew them all. He learned his way around the city.

He discovered commuter trains at age seven. These were more expensive than city buses, which would have made them impossible for Marco, who had no allowance—except that the trains had a policy that children eight and under could ride for free.

Now Marco rode out into the suburbs on winter weekends, bringing with him maps and train schedules for other cities and even countries to study. He made up itineraries for imaginary trips, running his finger along the thousands and thousands of miles of tracks and roads. Someday he would travel them all, this endless connected system of transportation. Librarians gave him funny looks when he took out travel books or an atlas, but he was polite and always returned them on time.

He would get off the trains at the end of the line, in another town, and wander around for hours in the cold bleak neighborhoods—walking kept him warmer than sitting in a cold house, and of course the trains were toasty—and then ride back. In the summer, when there was no school, he did it every day he could sneak away. He wandered through crowded, refreshingly air-conditioned suburban malls, and talked to the people who worked in the stores, asking them lots of questions. Marco was not shy, like Lilly.

He had a few friends from school, especially a boy named Nat, who liked to talk to Marco about science and space travel. Any kind of travel interested Marco. But mostly he preferred to ride the trains than to hang out with Nat.

Once he missed a train and came home late, and his parents were very worried and questioned him about it a lot, angry and suspicious. The experience made a permanent impression on him. So after that, he learned all the train schedules and routes, and how to change trains in different places, probably better than the conductors. He would fold up his map or close his guidebook, put it into his backpack, and step out onto the platform at just the exact time to catch the next train. The conductors got to know him too and sometimes even asked *him* about the schedules and routes. He became obsessed with always being right on time.

One kindly conductor named Nancy thought he was a genius. When he was too old to go for free, Nancy let him on anyway without making him pay, because she liked his stories about other countries so much, and she persuaded the other conductors to do the same. He enjoyed talking to them, and impressing them.

"Why do you go on buses and trains all the time, Marco?" Lilly asked him, one winter Saturday when he was twelve—it was too icy and windy that day for even Marco to go exploring. "You can trust me. I won't tell."

"How did you know?" he asked her, though her question didn't really surprise him. He had never told Lilly, or anybody else, what he was doing. He knew she had never followed him, because he never forgot to check when he left the house—but he always felt her staring at him when he returned from trips.

Lilly was frail and odd at eleven; their mother was always trying to get her to eat more, and taking her to Dr. Goldman, who gave her mental tests. Marco felt protective of Lilly—she was so delicate, almost otherworldly.

Now she looked down. "Don't tell. I try to hide it. But sometimes . . . I just know things," she said. "I knew where Dad left his briefcase."

Of course Marco remembered. A month ago, Dad was late for a meeting at work and couldn't find his briefcase. Suddenly Lilly blinked and said, "You left it at the office, on Mr. Branson's desk." Dad didn't believe her, and kept looking, but then he had to go. As soon as he got to work, he phoned. He *had* left it on Mr. Branson's desk.

Their parents hadn't been awed by this, like Marco. They had been worried. They worried about a lot of things, which was another reason Marco liked to get away.

They worried about money and about taking care of their big, old home. But they worried even more about Lilly, and he knew why. It was the biggest secret he kept from her. He had overheard them talking about it soon after the briefcase incident. He was up in the middle of the night to get a drink of water and walking quietly past their room. Their mother was crying. "She's just so much like Martha," she was saying. "Martha knew things too. And then she started going away. And . . ." Their mother could not go on.

"Look, Lilly's not going to disappear forever like Martha." Their father tried to comfort her. "We know what to watch for now. We won't let it happen again."

Marco hurried away then. He already knew that Martha was Mom's younger sister, who had an odd personality, and no friends, and had gone away for long periods of time without explanation. Then she never came back. This was before he was born. That was the reason for Dr. Goldman probing Lilly's mind—they were afraid the same thing would happen to Lilly. He swore to himself that he would never, never tell her. He knew she felt odd enough already. He seemed to be her only real friend. Suddenly he felt guilty about spending so much time away from her.

Now her eyes widened as he told her about all the different towns he went to and the people he talked to. There was something wonderful about describing his adventures to her. He knew she would never tell. "I need to get away from here," he said. "And I love to explore."

"But—where do you get the money?"

"Oh, sometimes I use lunch money," he said, shrugging, making light of it, because he knew Lilly felt bad that her doctors' bills ate up so much of their parents' money. "And the conductors let me take the trains for free," he added.

She seemed to feel better when she heard that. "Marco, I

wanted to ask if maybe . . . you could come with me to the basement. I know you won't be afraid of what I saw there. I'm scared to look at it alone."

"The basement? What did you see down there?"

"Come on, I'll show you . . . if you'll hold my hand."

CHAPTER ✸TWO

Marco and Lilly lived in a big old house that their great-grandparents had built in what had once been a fancy neighborhood. Now the carpets were threadbare, the roof leaked, and their parents couldn't afford to heat the rooms enough. But the children loved the house, with its dark paneled rooms and high ceilings and the big wooden staircase with the carved banister and the stained glass window on the landing.

But the basement was eerie. They rarely spent much time in it. Some basements have half windows that let in a little daylight; this basement was completely underground. They had to feel their way down the steep flight of wooden steps, because there was no light switch at the top. At the bottom, they had to grope in the dark, waving their hands above their heads, until they found the chain that turned on the bare ceiling bulb. Their father had tied a string to the chain, making it long enough so that Lilly, standing on her toes, could just reach it.

The giant furnace in the main room was like a black monster with long arms and legs, and now it seemed to be grumbling at them in its effort to warm part of the house. Next to it was an ancient washing machine with a hand-cranked wringer, which their mother never used; and trunks; and cardboard boxes and piles of magazines that they had finished reading.

"So what's down here? Why are you scared?" Marco asked Lilly.

"This way," she said, clinging to his hand.

Beyond a cement wall with an open door was another, smaller room. They had to grope their way in here too, reaching for the ceiling chain, also extended. Two of the walls in this room were made of stone, and there was a musty smell. Their mother said it had once been a root cellar, where people stored vegetables in the days before refrigeration. Now there was nothing in here but more cardboard boxes and an old worktable with newspapers piled on top and rusty tools covered with spiderwebs on the wall behind it.

"So where is it? The thing that scared you?"

Lilly was staring hard at the bare wall opposite the tools. He could feel her hand trembling as she clutched his. She turned to him in bewilderment. "You don't *see* it?" she said.

"See what?"

She pointed at the wall, a little irritably. *"That!"*

It was just an old stone wall, like it had always been. He shrugged. "A wall. Nothing scary about that."

"Those lights? Dim lights that make that tunnel there?" She sounded close to tears. "You don't see them? You don't have the feeling that something might come *out* of the tunnel? I lie awake at night thinking about it!" she said, her voice rising.

Marco squeezed her hand, trying to calm her. "I'm sorry, Lilly. I can't see it. You must be imagining—"

She stamped her foot, which was unusual for her—Lilly was a gentle person. "I *don't* imagine things. I know the difference—even if Dr. Goldman doesn't think so. Remember all the things? How I knew what Ruth wanted before she could talk and what was wrong whenever Dad was late from work? Oh, Marco! When I saw how brave and smart and adventurous you are, I thought maybe you could be the one to explore this tunnel. I . . . can't—and I'm not strong enough to stop them from coming through."

Now Marco was afraid too—but also intrigued. "How can I go down a tunnel if I can't even see it?" he objected.

"I didn't know you wouldn't be able to see it. But maybe if I show you exactly where it is, you can try."

Still clinging to his hand, Lilly stepped hesitantly toward the wall. "Here," she said, squatting down and pointing at, but not touching, a spot on the stone about two feet from the floor. "This is the right-hand edge of it."

Marco reached down with his left hand for the spot on the wall.

His finger sank into the stone, vanishing up to the knuckle.

He pulled his hand quickly back as if he had been burned—though he had felt nothing. "The wall isn't there!" he said, breathing hard. "I see it, but I don't feel it."

"That's the tunnel," Lilly said. "I told you."

Marco felt his heart thudding. He reached down again and put his hand to the right of the spot he had touched before. He felt stone. He moved his hand to the left. His whole hand went in, disappearing. This time he left it there for a moment. Nothing happened.

"You've got to let go of my hand, Lilly," he said. "I need both hands to feel the edges of it. But I'm still not promising anything."

Lilly reluctantly let go. Marco felt around with both

hands, tracing the edge of the emptiness. He went to the worktable, digging around in the newspapers until he found a blunt marking pencil.

Next to the pencil was an old, opened notebook with what looked like journal entries scribbled in it. The writing was too illegible to read. Marco was curious. Why was it here in the basement? Who had written it?

But the invisible hole in the wall was more amazing than an old notebook, which he couldn't read anyway. He hurried back to the wall and carefully, checking constantly by touch, drew an outline on the stone. The line he drew was about three feet high, and arched. He put the pencil back and stared at what he had drawn.

"Are you going through?" Lilly asked him. Her eyes were bright with fear but also excitement.

Marco was scared too. But what an adventure it might be! "I'll just *look* inside. And if I can see anything, and it looks safe—well, then I'll think about it."

He got to his knees and grasped the edge of the arch with both hands. He leaned forward and stuck his head into the wall. Lilly put her hand on his shoulder.

"Oh, wow!" he murmured.

He crawled into the stone.

CHAPTER THREE

The stone wall dissolved around him like smoke as he crawled downward from the dark basement into brilliant light. He was stopped by an invisible barrier for a moment, but then he felt Lilly's hand squeezing his leg, and the barrier melted away.

He saw a slow, slow, creeping world, like a movie being played one frame at a time.

And the first thing that struck his eye was something like a boat, with three creatures in it, hanging by cables at an impossible forty-five-degree angle. The cables were attached to a carved wooden crossbeam, supported by two posts about three stories high. As he watched, the world gradually speeded up—or he slowed down—and the boat began to fall, faster and faster. Strange, scratchy jangling music droned and then accelerated inside his head, rising in pitch. The boat flew up to the other end of its arc, then fell back again.

There were buildings and other creatures around the swinglike structure. Beyond them, something moved oddly in the distance. He had to find out what was going on!

Did he dare to go any closer?

He looked behind. He had to be sure he could get back.

There was only an alley, no sign of where he had come from. But his legs ended at the knees—he figured the rest of his legs must still be in the basement. He quickly crawled backward up into the basement again.

"Marco, why did you stay halfway inside the tunnel for so *long*?" Lilly said, gulping, close to tears again.

"So long?" Marco said, puzzled. "I was only there for a minute."

"No. You were just kneeling there without moving for like *twenty minutes*!" Lilly said.

"Twenty minutes? But that's crazy. It was only a minute. I hardly saw anything. How could it seem so much longer to you?"

"I don't understand," Lilly said. "What did you see?"

"Unbelievable," he said. "Some kind of city, some kind of

weird ride. Creatures. Music. Another world. But I have to make sure I can find my way back here."

He got an old cardboard box and a hammer from the worktable and crouched down on his knees again in front of the archway he had drawn.

"What's the box and the hammer for?" Lilly wanted to know.

"The box will show me where to come back, and the hammer will keep it from blowing away," he said. He was so excited now he was thinking he might actually sneak in a little closer. This was a lot more thrilling than the buses and trains, the suburbs and the malls.

"Marco, maybe you shouldn't go back after all," Lilly said. She grabbed his hand. "Don't go," she begged him. "It's okay. I'm not curious anymore."

"Now listen," he said gently, squeezing her hand. "Don't worry about me. I'll be fine. There just might be something a little crazy going on, about time or something. Be patient. Get a book. And don't worry. I'll just take another little look, and come right back as soon as possible. Look at what time it is when I leave, and when I come back." He checked his watch. It was five minutes past 1:00 P.M.

"But—"

"And I know you're curious too," he interrupted her. He crawled downward again, pushing the box in front of him.

This time he didn't turn back. He felt the barrier again, and Lilly's hand on his leg, and again the barrier dissolved.

He got slowly to his feet, feeling painfully heavy, his heart pounding with the effort. He slowly set the box behind him with the hammer inside it—it weighed more here—making sure that part of the box was invisible, meaning it was poking back into the basement. And then he took a good look around, the music speeding up in his ears.

He was in an alley, twenty yards away from a large open square surrounded by strangely shaped, drab buildings, and dust on the ground. Shiny, purplish creatures, some about his size and some smaller, were speeding up from slow motion to normal speed—though now he was sure what was happening was that he was slowing down.

The creatures crowded around the edges of the square, creatures like insects with six limbs and ridged, carapaced heads. It was horrifying, disgusting, to see insectlike creatures so large. He felt the urge to turn and run.

But they were watching the swing, and hadn't noticed him. He stayed in the alley, peeking out from behind the corner of a building.

The swing rose and fell in increasingly high arcs, creaking. The creatures inside it were rocking energetically back and forth, clearly trying to get it to go as high as possible. Was it an amusement park ride? Was it a contest? The creatures watching were exchanging small objects. Money? Were they making bets?

And behind the village, far away, a peculiar blistering light, like a kind of tangled explosion, spinning wildly, constantly changing. It reminded him of a picture he had seen in one of Nat's astronomy books, but at the moment he couldn't place it exactly. It was too far away to see very well—and it hurt his eyes to look at it anyway.

Again, he controlled a sudden urge to turn back. He knew he had to hurry—a long time might be going by in the basement and Lilly was waiting there, alone and afraid. But scared as he was, he wanted to get a closer look at the creatures and what they were doing. He moved forward carefully, sweating, his knees unsteady under his unexpected weight. Gravity on this world was stronger than on Earth. Whenever one of the creatures seemed about to look in his direction, he lurched behind a wall and froze.

They constantly moved their heads slightly back and forth. He couldn't see any eyes on them. Perhaps their sense of sight was somehow different from human beings'.

He concentrated on looking at the creatures, and did his best to keep his eyes away from the distant monstrous thing behind them.

Suddenly a creature at a booth glanced directly at him.

Again he froze, his heart pounding in his neck. He started to turn to run away.

But the creature didn't threaten him. It bowed politely, putting its two front limbs to its forehead and lowering its head. *Greetings. Have you eaten yet? That will be five ticals to get inside.*

He clapped his hands over his ears. It wasn't words exactly that were entering his brain, drowning out his own thoughts, but feelings, meanings. And somehow he was absolutely sure they were coming from the creature. There was a bored, superior attitude toward Marco that came through clearly, despite the polite gesture. But still no inkling of a threat.

"Huh?" he said. He was a little less frightened now, and relaxed slightly. It didn't seem to want to eat him, it just wanted money. He figured the safest thing was to be polite himself. *Greetings,* he thought, without going any closer, and bowed like the creature had. *What is a tical? I don't have any—*

The creature made the mental equivalent of a disdainful sniff. *Then I'm afraid you will have to go away and leave me—*

Then the creature jerked and took a sudden, alarmed step backward. *Why . . . it is Marco! The older brother of Lilly!*

Every other creature turned and looked at him. Even the creatures on the giant swing stared, and stopped pumping. The larger ones seemed suddenly frozen. The smaller ones scuttled back and forth excitedly. Children? Marco wondered despite a growing feeling of panic.

He wanted to run for real now, but he was just too amazed. *You know Lilly?* Marco thought at them.

We are sending *for Lilly!* Marco sensed that they were all communicating with him at once. *We need Lilly. We need her very, very much. The ceremony can proceed without her, yes. But with her, it will be so much more effective, so much more pleasing to The Unknowable.*

What on earth were they talking about? He looked at his watch. It was 1:13. *I have to get back now,* he told them, starting to turn away.

Please bring Lilly here! We need her. Bring her back next time.

He had seen enough. He didn't want to get any closer. And—fascinating as this was—it was too weird and frightening. He wouldn't be coming back here again.

He turned and almost ran for the box—he was too heavy to really run—and, he was very glad to see, the box was still just where he had left it.

Do not be afraid! Tell Lilly to come soon. She is the one we need. We must teach her how to be polite, and other things too! cried the voices in his head.

Marco reached the box. He got down on his knees and pushed it forward, in the direction where part of it was invisible. He emerged into the basement. He could hardly see, it was so much darker here. But it was wonderful to feel the great weight lifting from him.

And then Lilly's hands were on his shoulders, pulling him forward. "Oh, Marco, you came back! You came back!" She hugged him.

He squirmed away and looked at his watch, squinting in the dim light. It was just about 1:14. Nine minutes had gone by since he had left the basement.

"I was getting so worried," Lilly said. "I didn't know what I could tell them if you weren't back in time for supper. What was down there?"

"What time is it?"

"After four."

He shook his head. "Well, it's a good thing I'm never going back there again. I was only there for nine minutes, but three hours went by back here. If I spent any time there at all, Mom and Dad would start missing me here for sure. Lucky I came back when I did."

"And lucky Ruth went upstairs before you came back," said Lilly.

Marco felt a pang. Ruth was seven now, sturdy, curious, and a tattletale. "What did you tell her? How did you get her to go away?" Marco asked. He began piling up boxes to hide the arch.

"Well, you know how she's always following me around,

and wanting attention," Lilly said. "She asked what I was doing and I said I liked reading here." Lilly was good at imitating Ruth's voice. "She said, 'Why are you reading down on the dirty cold floor? You're being cuckoo again! I'm telling Mommy!' That was a while ago. Maybe she forgot about it and didn't tell Mom. I hope so." Lilly looked behind Marco and shivered. "What did you see there?"

He looked back at the wall. "Are the lights still going?"

She nodded unhappily. "I can see them through the boxes. What was down there? Was there anything that could . . . come through?"

He told her what he had seen. But when it came to the part about how they were sending for her, how they needed and wanted her, he looked away, and left all that out. He was protective of her.

She listened, squeezing his hand. "What if one of those creatures tried to follow you?" she asked.

"I don't think they could. There was nothing out there that showed where the tunnel to the basement *is*. I only found it because of the box I brought with me, and now the box isn't there anymore."

"Yeah, but . . . they knew our names," she pointed out. "If they can know something like that, then maybe they can know how to get here too. Maybe they spied on us."

He sighed, feeling unsure. "They don't want to come here. What they want is for—" He was about to tell her they wanted *her* to go *there,* but stopped himself. "I wish you wouldn't be so afraid, Lilly. They were busy having their ceremony or their giant swing contest or whatever. They didn't try to follow me or anything. They told *me* to come back, like there was no way they were going to come here. Don't worry. We just won't come down here anymore."

"But . . ."

"Okay, they were weird looking. But they weren't threatening in any way, or even curious. They talked about being *polite*! I wasn't really afraid of them," he said, which wasn't exactly true. "It was that thing like a spinning bunch of neon lights behind them that was so terrible. And there's no way that could get through here."

Lilly relaxed a little. He knew that she trusted and believed him.

But Marco worried about what he hadn't told her.

"What have you two been doing down here for so long?" their mother said behind them, and they both jumped. "And I didn't know you were down here too, Marco. Ruth said it was only Lilly. You're hiding out down here instead of taking care of her, young lady." But she sounded more frightened than angry.

"Er," Lilly said. "Well . . . I mean—"

"We're playing mind-reading games," Marco interrupted her. Feeling brave because of the adventure he had just been through, he dared to add, "Do you always believe everything Ruth tells you?"

"Now don't go blaming that little child because of your own . . ." Their mother paused, and sighed. "Well, I have to admit, I'm not happy about that tattletale side of her," she said. "But I still don't understand what you—"

There was a crash from upstairs. "Oh, what's she gotten into now?" their mother said, and turned and hurried for the stairs. "Come and help me!" she called back to Lilly.

"Like I said, it's a good thing I'm never going back there again," Marco said.

But Lilly knew he was wrong about that.

CHAPTER ✷FOUR

"Bills, bills." Their father sighed gloomily as they sat down to dinner that night.

"Now don't bring problems to the dinner table," their mother said. But she didn't look too happy herself. They were eating canned beans and hot dogs again.

Lilly felt guilty. She knew the bills from Dr. Goldman were very high—Dr. Goldman, who was always giving her those tricky tests and asking her unpleasant questions about why she had no friends. She wished she could just stop going to her, but her mother insisted. She hated it that

Marco and Ruth were deprived of things they wanted because of her doctor's bills.

Their father worked for a small company and he didn't make much money. Their mother couldn't get a real job because of Ruth—they couldn't afford a baby-sitter or day care—so Mom stayed at home doing piecework jobs. But she was so busy taking care of Ruth and the house that she didn't have time to do as much work as she would have liked.

"Can I have another hot dog?" Ruth asked.

"I'm sorry, honey, that's all there is," their mother said. "There's Popsicles for dessert," she added brightly.

"You can have mine too," Lilly offered, knowing Ruth would want more than one.

Ruth just looked at her, wide-eyed and happy. Lilly knew Ruth craved her attention—it was why she had followed her to the basement. It made her feel better to be able to give her the Popsicle.

If their mother hadn't inherited the house, they certainly would have lived someplace smaller, someplace not so expensive to keep up. But despite the constant wrenching struggle about money, Lilly would have hated to live in a little boring modern house. They had fewer clothes than most of the kids at school, and their family had only one old car, and they didn't eat roast beef and steak like other families. But Lilly still preferred living in this house.

And now our basement is a doorway to somewhere magic, Lilly thought. She was still scared something might come through, but also deeply thrilled that she had discovered something so miraculous, something no one else could see.

It was Lilly's job to put Ruth to bed every night so Mom could work. Lilly read to her from library books, which Ruth tolerated because she liked the attention from Lilly. But she would have vastly preferred to be watching TV, and tonight she was hungry, which made her irritable. She fidgeted while Lilly read, and sighed and barely bothered to look at the pictures.

Finally, Lilly said, "What's the matter, Ruth? Would you like me to read you another book? How about—"

"A book is the same all the time, but TV is different every night," Ruth complained for the hundredth time.

Lilly knew that if it weren't for her, they probably *would* have a TV. "I'm sorry, honey," she said, as she did every night. "I can't help it. I'll get you new books from the library. Every book is different too."

"I don't like books," Ruth said. "I want to watch TV."

Lilly's shoulders sagged. She felt tired. "What if I tell you a story?" she said.

"Like a story about what you were *really* doing down in the basement today?" Ruth suggested, her voice brightening.

Lilly stiffened. She didn't want Ruth going down into the basement—she might see Marco going in or coming out of the tunnel, and then everything would be ruined. "Okay, I'll tell you a story about the basement," Lilly said. "A *true* story." She thought fast. Then she dropped her voice to a whisper. "This has to be a secret between us. Mommy and Daddy don't want anybody to know about this. If they find out you know, they'll be very angry at you, and no Popsicles for a month."

"Then how do *you* know?" Ruth asked her. She could be suspicious, but she was also curious—it ran in the family— and she was still, fortunately, young enough to be gullible.

"I overheard them talking about it once. They don't know I know. If you tell them, they'll be mad, and I'll never tell you anything secret again in my life," Lilly said very firmly. She hoped the threat would work—she knew the bond between them was very important to Ruth.

"Okay, tell me! I promise I won't tell!" Ruth said.

"Do you swear it forever?" Lilly asked her, holding up her right hand and staring hard at her.

"Okay, I swear it!" Ruth said impatiently, holding up her right hand too. "Now tell me!"

"A little girl disappeared in the basement," Lilly said quietly. She felt bad about doing this, but keeping the tunnel secret was terribly important, and the only way to do that was to scare Ruth away.

And then she thought of something. Aunt Martha had grown up in this house. And Aunt Martha had disappeared forever before they were born. She didn't think it had been in the basement, but Lilly could make that part up.

"Mom and Dad don't talk much about Aunt Martha, Mom's little sister. But she grew up in this house and she loved going down to the basement. And one day she went down there—and never came back."

Ruth was breathing hard. "But aren't *you* afraid of going down there, then?"

How was she going to deal with this one? "Er, I would be, except I'm the older sister. Mom was the older sister and went down there all the time and never had a problem. It was her *younger* sister who disappeared in the basement."

"The younger sister went down there and never came back?" Ruth repeated slowly.

"It's only dangerous for the younger sister," Lilly confirmed, feeling worse than ever, but still determined.

"I . . . I want to go to bed now," Ruth said, about to start crying. "Up here, in my room, where it's safe." And she dove under the covers.

Before Lilly went to bed, she told Marco about scaring Ruth away from the basement. "Er, that's brilliant, Lilly," he told her, looking a little ashen. Lilly was surprised. She didn't think scaring Ruth would bother *him*. "I wish I could have seen her face when she ran into bed. Er . . . except I'm never going down that tunnel again, you know."

"I know," Lilly said, not believing a word of it.

"But still—anything to keep her scared and away from there is smart," Marco agreed. "It can be a kind of game we play with her—a game she doesn't know is a game."

Lilly had a very vivid dream that night. She dreamed that *she* crawled through the tunnel in the basement, the tunnel that only she could see. And the world on the other side was a lot like Marco had described it. But why hadn't he told her how beautiful it was?

The music, for instance. It wasn't just scratchy and jangling, as Marco had said. It was the loveliest, most joyous sound she had ever heard. Why hadn't Marco cried—as she was crying—to be privileged to hear such a thing?

Why hadn't he told her about all the gardens and brightly colored flowers in the village? Why hadn't he told her more about the beautiful buildings in the square, and the temple behind them, covered with gold and sparkling multicolored stones?

And there was no terrible jolting thing far away on the horizon that hurt her eyes to look at. Had Marco made that up?

Especially he hadn't told her how friendly the creatures were, how clearly benign, despite their insectlike appearance. They bowed to her repeatedly, and she bowed back. They showered her with thoughts about how special she was, how much stronger her mental powers were than other humans'. They wanted her, they needed her, more than Ruth did, more than anyone ever had before in her life. It was an irresistible feeling.

She woke up abruptly in the middle of the night, in her cold dark room in the winter. It was summer in that other world, and always warm. And she was special, unique, marvelous over there, not just a frail, sickly little girl who was too shy to have any friends except her brother.

And now she realized she had been having dreams like this for years. She had just never remembered them until now, when the tunnel had appeared.

She almost felt like crawling through the tunnel herself. Now.

She shrank back against the pillow, pulling the covers around her. No. She was still too afraid, despite the dream. If she ever went there at all—and she was still extremely doubtful about that—it would have to be with Marco. Never alone. Even though the dream was so wonderful.

"Marco, why didn't you tell me what it was really like in that other world?" she asked him the next day, Sunday, after their breakfast of cold cereal.

"I did tell you," Marco insisted, but his eyes slid away from her and she knew, absolutely, that he had left something out. "What makes you think I didn't tell you?"

"I dreamed about it last night. There were gardens and flowers all over the place. The music was so lovely, it was like heaven. There was no horrible craziness in the distance that hurt my eyes. And the buildings and the temple were so beautiful, covered with gold, with colored banners and streamers everywhere."

Marco shook his head. "That was a dream, Lilly. It makes sense that you would dream about it and it makes sense it would be unreal in the dream. Dreams are never like reality. You know that."

"And they needed me," she went on, ignoring him. "They said I was special, there was nobody else like me, it was *me* they needed and wanted more than anybody else."

"They told you that, in the dream?"

She nodded vehemently.

"It was a dream, Lilly," Marco said firmly. "They told me

to come back there and learn how to be polite. But they didn't . . . they didn't say anything about you."

Now he was lying, she could tell. He had never lied to her before. What was he hiding from her, and why?

"Take me down there now," she said. "I'm not afraid anymore."

CHAPTER FIVE

Lilly had never sounded so sure of herself. "I'm the one who can *see* the tunnel. It must be meant for me. I have the right to go through it if I want."

He sighed. What was he going to do? He feared for her safety.

"Take me there. Now," she said, uncharacteristically forceful. "Ruth's next door at Sally's. Dad has the Sunday paper, Mom's working. They won't notice if we're gone now. And I'm the one who can see the tunnel. It's meant for me."

Why was she being like this? He thought of how she was

at school, one grade behind him, always alone there, ignored by the other girls—and too timid to approach them. What had done this to her? Was it possible that what she had experienced hadn't just been a dream? Had the creatures somehow communicated directly with her?

Would it be wrong of him *not* to take her? What she said about being able to see the tunnel made sense. And he remembered the barrier he had felt, which had only dissolved when she was touching him. There would probably be no barrier for her.

But he couldn't imagine her in that place. It wasn't pretty, as she had dreamed it. Had they portrayed it that way in order to lure her there? What did they want with her? If he brought her there, would they ever let her go?

Marco reasoned with himself. He knew her very well. She was too timid to stay there long enough for the creatures to trap her. Anyway, he wouldn't let that happen. He'd give her a peek at the place, to quiet her down and show her that her dream was wrong, and then drag her back.

The phone rang and Marco ran to answer it, half hoping for an excuse not to take Lilly. It was his friend Nat, asking him to go to a Sunday matinee—Nat often asked him to do things, and sometimes Marco went with him. Marco was on the verge of agreeing to go—but then he just couldn't. He knew how important it was to Lilly for him to take her through the tunnel now.

"Okay, come on, let's get this over with," he said grimly to Lilly.

"You don't have to be mad at me," she said, on the way down to the basement. "It was you who lied, not me. Why did you make up that part about that horrible light in the distance that never stopped spinning or erupting or whatever?"

And then it clicked. Hearing Lilly's description and talking to Nat reminded him of a book his friend had shared with him about black holes. In it was a simulated picture that looked like that terrible thing. It was a picture of a naked singularity.

Everybody knew about black holes. They were stars that died and collapsed down to a tiny point called a singularity. Because the singularity was so dense, its gravitational pull was incredibly powerful—so powerful that not even light, the fastest thing in the universe, could escape from it, once it got close enough. That's why the radius around the singularity was called a black hole.

But scientists had recently discovered that under certain conditions, such as if the star was spinning fast enough (many stars rotated, just as the earth did), the black hole might not form around the singularity. These rare objects—nobody knew if they actually existed—were known as naked singularities, because they were not clothed and hidden in a black hole. They were visible. And light could escape from them, light bent into twisted convoluted paths by the powerful gravitational tidal forces, and the spin. Scientists speculated that singularities created wormholes—tunnels through another dimension—that connected to other universes. And if there was one thing Nat had told Marco that truly thrilled him, it was that there were almost certainly an infinite number of universes, according to the tenets of quantum mechanics.

Some scientists also believed that naked singularities could be the cause of the end of the universe—one or many. Naked singularities were highly unstable. Because of their almost unimaginable gravity, as well as the spin, they could get out of control and sometimes explode. If that happened, it could cause a chain reaction that could spread through more than one universe.

Marco and Lilly were standing in front of the wall with the tunnel and its pile of boxes. "Marco, are you really mad at me?" Lilly asked.

"Shhh! I'm thinking," he told her as he moved the boxes aside.

Gravity did something else too: It slowed down time. This was an accepted scientific fact that had been proven by Einstein at the beginning of the century. Any object approaching a singularity would go slower and slower. But it wouldn't feel any different to the object. From the object's point of view, it would seem as though the rest of the universe had speeded up.

Marco felt his heart begin to race. That was the explanation for everything! The slow world was in the vicinity of a naked singularity. That's why gravity was stronger there, and that's why time went slower there too. It made complete scientific sense. Now he was excited about the place all over again. Nat would be so envious if he knew; Marco was the first person in the world to see an actual naked singularity, not just a simulation.

He got the box with the hammer in it and knelt down beside the arch he had drawn on the wall. Horrible as it was, now he wanted to see the naked singularity again with his own eyes.

Lilly knelt down behind him, her hand on the cuff of his pants. He could feel her hand trembling. "You don't have to come, you know," he said.

"Go on," Lilly said.

Marco pushed the box ahead of him and moved into the tunnel. This time he felt no barrier at all. He noticed Lilly letting go of him before he got all the way through. That was fine. Maybe she wouldn't come after all. He was afraid of what the creatures would do if they sensed her there. He went through alone.

He saw the slow world gradually accelerate as he entered it. Before he went any farther he made sure the box was still half invisible, still partly in the basement tunnel. He couldn't see Lilly, but it sure seemed like she wasn't coming. "Whatever happens, leave the box exactly where it is!"

he shouted back at her, hoping she could hear, hoping she would stay where she was. He got up with difficulty in the stronger gravity and looked around.

The swing ceremony was still going on. How much time had passed here since he had come the day before? An hour or less?

There were the drab buildings, the dust. The giant swing was moving faster and higher now. The onlookers waved and cheered, urging on the athletes, their heads twitching back and forth as always. He could now see that at one side of the supporting structure of the swing was a tall pole, with a little bag hanging way at the top of it. The creature in the swing closest to the pole was reaching for the bag, the others rocking harder so that it could get close enough to grab it. The creature was very high and leaning way out over the edge of the swing now. It could fall at any instant—and from that height it would mean death for sure. What was in the bag? Why did they want it so much? What was this ceremony for?

He was a little afraid to, but he couldn't help looking at something else for a moment. His eyes moved past the swing and the creatures to the thing in the distance.

There was the spinning, erupting frenzy of the singularity, the reason for the gravity, the reason for the slow motion here. How far away was it? How close would you have to be to get sucked into it?

The creatures turned from watching the swing and bowed to him. *Greetings, Marco! Have you eaten yet?*

He bowed back.

Where is Lilly? We thought she was coming with you this time. You keep senselessly rushing in and out of your world and not bringing her. We need her. We need her more than ever. The danger is very great now, to our world, and to many of the worlds it touches.

Lilly isn't coming through. She'll never come through. Stop sending her those lying messages, he thought.

Do not be so hot-hearted. You must learn to be polite, and cool-headed. Otherwise you will make many mistakes. We can help you a lot if you will bring Lilly to us. We will show you how to go everywhere, everywhere there is to go.

What did that mean? If it meant what it sounded like, it was very tempting. But he didn't like the part about bringing Lilly to them.

The swing rose up very close to the pole and the creature on the end of it made a wild grab for the bag, and only barely managed to stay inside the boat. A roar went up from the crowd. Marco turned and waddled for the box.

Lilly had hesitated, suddenly afraid again. She wanted to get a good look before she went through.

She watched Marco pushing the box ahead of him into

the light. She saw the corner of a building. And Marco crept slower, and slower, and slower.

She wasn't ready to go through, she didn't dare. The way Marco had slowed down was too terrifying. She moved back and waited at the edge of the tunnel, in the basement, watching the lights. She did keep looking around to be sure Ruth wasn't coming down, but she hadn't heard the front door open and close, so she felt pretty safe about that.

Finally, after about three hours, Marco was slowly pushing the box back ahead of him toward her. He began to speed up.

Lilly got out of the way as Marco came through, panting.

"You were smart . . . not to go," he said.

"It was so slow. That's the part that scared me. Could you feel it?"

He shook his head. "It always feels normal to me when I'm there. That's how these things work. What time is it?"

"Almost two. You went in at ten-thirty." She sighed. "I wanted to go through, but I just couldn't. What did you see? Was it like my dream?"

He shook his head. "It wasn't like your dream. I saw what was really there. The old buildings, the dust, the naked singularity—that's what that light thing is called, and it's the reason for everything weird there. And I saw that horrible swing ceremony. I wonder if creatures die on that thing?" He shuddered. "And the creatures *do* want you. They tried to bribe me to bring you to them. They said there was great danger if I didn't. They said they would show me how to go everywhere there is to go, if I brought you. But I won't. I never will. We're never going back there again, either of us."

"But why do you and I see that world so differently?" she asked, realizing Marco was telling the truth about what he saw. "What does that mean?"

Marco shook his head. "I don't know. And that's why I don't like that place. Okay, I understand why it goes slower and why it feels heavier, and I can explain that to you. But I don't like it that they're lying to you about what it's like. I don't trust them. And that's why I don't want to go back." He paused. "We should close the door to this room and never open it again."

"I guess you're right," Lilly said. But she felt sad. The sensation in her dream of being needed had been so real, and so wonderful.

Marco hadn't really meant what he said about neither of them going through again. He wanted what the creatures had offered—to be able to go everywhere. But he wanted it without bringing Lilly to them.

He tried it without her after school the next day, when Lilly was upstairs taking care of Ruth.

He couldn't get through. Without her, the barrier stopped him completely. There he crouched, looking at the slow, slow, creeping world on the other side, and unable to reach it. It seemed that her touch was necessary for him to get past the barrier.

Was there any way he could get through without her?

It didn't take him long to get an idea. He found her hair-brush in the upstairs bathroom and pulled off some dark strands. Then he thought of something else and got the alarm clock from beside his bed. He hurried down to the basement again.

He set the alarm clock just outside the archway drawn on the stone wall. It was 3:30 P.M. on the clock and on his watch. He put Lilly's hair in his pocket and knelt down in front of the box.

And pushed the box all the way through. Her hair had dissolved the barrier.

He stopped and waited before he approached the crea-tures. The swing was just reaching the top of its arc. The creature in front, leaning way, way out of the swing, made a wild grab for the bag.

And fell, tumbling through the air.

There was a roar from the crowd, which covered what-ever terrible sound the creature made when it hit the ground and its carapace cracked open like an eggshell. Marco put his hand over his mouth and closed his eyes, feeling sick, wanting to get out of there now.

But somehow he couldn't leave. And the creatures acted fast. Immediately two of them were carrying the dead crea-ture away in a kind of stretcher around to the back of a building.

All the rest of the creatures prostrated themselves in the direction of the singularity, deeper than their normal bow, kneeling down on the ground. And it seemed to Marco that the singularity changed, becoming just perceptibly calmer and less violent. But it had to be his imagination. A creature's death couldn't possibly have any effect on it!

He had to ask about the death, even though he knew time was flying by back at home and he had to hurry. He limped in the high gravity toward the closest creature—they were all getting up now. He had felt before that they were all thinking at him at once. Communicating with one of them would be the same as communicating with all of them.

Greetings, Marco thought at it, and bowed. And then he remembered to add, *Have you eaten yet?* He didn't know why they always asked that, but it was part of their politeness ritual.

The creature returned the greeting. *Very nice to see you, Marco. But where is Lilly? It is Lilly we need. How did you get through without her?*

Lilly, Lilly, Lilly!

He wanted to ask about the death, still feeling stunned, but suddenly he was shy about it. Death was out of his experience, not something he talked about with people on the trains.

Then he had an idea. *I have something of Lilly's. Something maybe you want. I'll give it to you . . . if you promise to show me what you said about how to go everywhere.*

The creature's eyeless, twitching, insectlike head could not make readable expressions. But Marco sensed a moment of confusion. *Strands of the fur from her head?* it thought questioningly.

How did you— Marco started to ask it, and then stopped. Of course it would know. It could read his thoughts.

We have to think about it. And to answer the other question on your mind—the unfortunate swing rider fell to his death. The risk is necessary, or the ceremony would have no meaning, no effect. Anyway, the swing riders are of the lowest class.

Lowest class? What did that mean? *But . . .* Marco looked frantically at his watch, his mind bursting with more questions. *I have to get back. No time now. Maybe you can tell me next time if you can use her hair.* He hurried as quickly as he could for the box.

His watch said 3:32 when he emerged into the basement. The alarm clock told him it was 4:12. Two minutes had gone by in the other world, and forty-two minutes had gone by at home. It wasn't perfectly neat and exact, but it was approximately twenty-one to one. At least he knew that now, and could plan his time over there accordingly.

But he felt very disheartened. The time difference was so great that anything he did over there would have to be really fast, or his parents would have the police out looking for him. How could the creatures teach him to go everywhere there was to go in so little time?

Lilly kept watching him at dinner. How much did she know about what was going on in his mind? He didn't think she could read it *exactly*, like the creatures did. But she could probably tell he was keeping something from her. And it wouldn't be hard for her to guess what it was.

She stared at him silently throughout the evening. It made him very uncomfortable. No wonder she had no friends, he thought irritably, if she acted that way with the kids at school.

He also felt more frightened now. The creatures weren't actually threatening to him. But after bowing at the singularity, they hadn't seemed to care very much that one of their own had died. What kind of beings could they be to attach so much importance to a ceremony that often resulted in death?

Beings like people, he suddenly realized. Like the ancient Romans and their gladiators. Like bullfights. Like war. But did being like people make the creatures any the less frightening?

"Lilly, why are you staring at Marco like that?" Ruth

wanted to know. She seemed to be jealous that Lilly wasn't paying more attention to her.

Marco waited until his parents had gone to bed at 11:00 P.M. That gave him eight hours until they got up at seven. That was 480 minutes. Dividing that by twenty-one gave him barely twenty-three minutes in the other world. He groaned. What could he learn in twenty-three minutes? To stay there for any decent length of time he would have to vanish from home for days. Was it even worth trying, and losing a night's sleep? He should probably give up on the whole thing.

He was too excited not to try. He hurried down to the basement and through the tunnel.

A new group was climbing into the giant swing now—the deadly ceremony was still going on. Large numbers of individuals clustered on flimsy little balconies with low railings, high in the air, that seemed far too precarious for them. Even the audience was in danger. Didn't death mean anything to these creatures?

But he didn't have time to worry about that now. He quickly went through the greeting ritual with the first crea-ture he saw, and then thought, *For Lilly's hair, will you show me how to go everywhere?*

Lilly is so special that even the fur from her head will help us. And to go everywhere—you can only get that by making the pilgrimage to The Unknowable, and retrieving what was stolen.

Somehow he knew what "The Unknowable" was—the naked singularity. He looked over at it, spinning and pulsing, spitting out sparks of all colors, more violent than ever now. *I have to go there? To that thing?* he asked, pointing at it, horrified.

Put down your limb! the creature said, stepping back in alarm. *Pointing at The Unknowable! We have to take back what we said we would do for—*

Marco put his hand down instantly. *I didn't know! We don't know about these things where I come from. I'm only a kid. Please?*

Marco looked at his watch. Four minutes had gone by. Eighteen to go.

Well . . . We are kindhearted. And we want the fur from Lilly's head. We forgive you—this once. But do not forget.

Okay, okay, I never will again, I promise. Now, how do we do all this? I only have seventeen minutes.

Other creatures had gathered around them now. Their bodies were about the height of his waist, but when they stood up and raised their front limbs, their heads were the same height as his. Now they swayed backward and forward on their four hind limbs, overcome by some emotion.

Were they laughing? *What's the matter?* Marco asked them.

Seventeen minutes? A very funny joke. Give us the fur from Lilly's head before you speak any more nonsense.

Will you keep your promise to me?

We keep our promises. Now you keep yours.

For the first time in any of his contact with the creatures he felt a threatening tone in their thought patterns. He pulled the small bundle of hairs out of his pocket and handed it over.

The creature accepted it reverently in its front pincers. The others clustered around. Then they all turned away from Marco and scurried off.

Wait a minute! Where are you going? What about your promise? he asked them.

We take this to the altar first—a place where you are not allowed. It will help to forestall the disaster that is coming—to our world and yours too. After that ceremony, we will come back and explain more to you.

How long will the ceremony take?

Only an hour, by your reckoning here.

There was no way he was going to learn anything now. He had only fifteen minutes left here before it would be 7:00 A.M. at home. He might as well go back now, and get a little sleep.

Oh, yes. The giant swing ceremony will pause for now.

But you will have to win that too, if you want to learn what you ask.

The giant swing ceremony? How could he ever dare to do that?

He might as well accept the fact that learning anything from them was hopeless. The tests were too frightening and difficult. And he would never have enough time here. He pushed the box back into the basement. The alarm clock showed 1:48.

CHAPTER SEVEN

The dream came to Lilly just as Marco was crawling into bed.

Six of the creatures, glowing benignly, crouched around her. She was lying on a low stone table. She was not afraid, because she knew they would never harm her.

Lilly, we need you to help us. We need you to be part of the three-in-one. We have lost our other human contact.

Here she sensed they were leaving something out, but they went on too quickly for her to ask what it was.

The Unknowable, The Lord. We have no medium now to communicate with It. Only a special person from your world can appease it—we have tried, and we do not have that ability. And so now our religion forbids us from trying. But we cannot go on for long without this communication—the three-in-one. The Unknowable will soon become dangerous—to our world, and your world too. You could be the medium to appease it. Your brother is special too, but more limited than you. He cannot do it on his own. If you cannot come through to us, if you cannot face The Unknowable yourself, then you must help your brother. We will tell you what you can do.

What are you leaving out? she dared to ask them. *What happened to your other human contact?*

There was a pause, a sudden blockage of all thought patterns from them, a wall. What were they hiding from her? Now she was uneasy—now she did feel afraid, because they were keeping secrets from her. And in the dream state she was not timid as she was in the real world.

I can't help you unless you tell me about your last human contact, the other medium, the last part of the three-in-one. What are you hiding?

Again there was hesitation. Then—within a frame of deep reluctance—she received a brief flash, a sudden image of a young woman sitting on a red-and-blue carpet, her hand resting protectively on a strange metal box in front of her. The woman looked oddly familiar, like someone Lilly had seen in a photograph, long ago. But in the dream state she could not pinpoint where she had ever seen the photograph. The woman was smiling mysteriously.

The image vanished.

We can show you no more than that. You must trust us. For yourself and your brother. For the future of you and your family. And for us too. To save our worlds from The Unknowable. The Unknowable is only barely under control, even at the best of times. When it really erupts it will destroy us, and the destruction will carry over to your world, and many of the worlds we are connected to. That is why we made the tunnel and the lights for you to see it. We are performing the giant swing ceremony night and day, but it is not enough now. Lilly. We appeal to you. You must help us.

How can I help you? Marco is so much stronger and braver and—

He cannot do it on his own. He cannot do it without you. You can tell him and help him.

What was she going to have to do?

Then they told her more. And she was even more frightened.

CHAPTER EIGHT

They walked to school together the next morning, Tuesday. It was snowing. They were silent until she said, "You got through last night without me there to break the barrier."

He turned and looked at her, astonished. He knew there was no point in lying to Lilly—not telling her something was one thing; lying was entirely different. "How did you know?" he asked her.

"I had a dream. Not an ordinary dream. It was like the other dreams I had about the creatures over there."

"The lying dreams," Marco muttered.

"Was it a lie that you got through by taking hair from

my brush?" she asked him. "Was it a lie that they offered to teach you how to go anywhere—except that you have to do some very hard things first? Worse than hard things. Impossible things. Impossible—without me."

"Did they tell you that in the dream?" He couldn't help feeling resentful that they told her he couldn't do it on his own.

"Yes. And they told me other things." Her voice dropped. "Scary things."

"What scary things?" he asked, wondering if he really wanted to know.

"They need me to be some kind of medium to be in contact with this thing they call The Unknowable, or The Lord. Or else it will destroy everything. But I don't think—"

"The Unknowable! That's what they call the naked singularity. Did they show it to you this time?"

"No, they didn't show it to me. But if I dared to go through there, I could contact it directly. But . . ." She shook her head, and her thin shoulders sagged beneath her snow-covered brown wool coat. "I just don't think I can do that kind of thing. I don't have the strength—or the guts. And Ruth wouldn't leave me alone long enough even if I did!" And now Marco sensed that Lilly resented her own timidity as well as being tied down to Ruth—she felt sad because she couldn't be the one to go.

"I think it has to be you, with my help." Lilly made an

attempt to brighten a little. "We have to be part of what they call the three-in-one. And then you'll learn the thing you want to know, about how to go everywhere. So, the first thing we have to figure out is, how you can go away—for a longer time. And . . ." She paused, chewing on her lip. "It has to be soon. As soon as possible."

He didn't like the sound of that. "Why does it have to be as soon as possible?"

"Because no one will be safe until you do—us or them."

"Us too?" he repeated stupidly. That was a stunner. The slow world—he had always seen it as being safely tucked away on the other side of the barrier in the basement. It wasn't easy to get through from this side—and on the other side, the tunnel to this world was invisible. Sure, it was dangerous over *there*. But he had never believed that the danger could make its way over here, to this world.

But that's what Lilly had been afraid of. From the beginning. And Lilly could feel and see things that nobody else could see.

But he didn't want to believe it. "Oh, come on. How can we be in danger? It was just a silly dream again—"

"A dream that told me you went over there last night, with my hair, and gave it to them, so that they would teach you how to go everywhere there is to go. Is that true or not?"

He sighed. "Yeah, that part was true." And he knew it was also true what some scientists believed about the danger of naked singularities. He couldn't avoid it anymore.

"And the rest is true too," she asserted. "That thing you call the naked singularity. Well, it does exist. And we're not safe from it either. If it erupts, it will blow up their world and ours, because we're connected. They need me to appease it. And—if I don't go over there and do it myself—I have to do it through you. Meaning you have to go over there. And stay for a while."

"But that's not possible," he argued, wanting to delay the decision to go. "Staying over there for any length of time would mean I'd be missed back here. Little things like Mom and Dad and school might notice, you know?"

"Yeah," she said. "You don't think I know that? You don't think I know that's the first problem we have to solve?"

They had reached school, and the bell was ringing. Kids thronged around them. "Talk to you later," Lilly said softly, already drawing into herself, turning into the shy, almost speechless person she became around other children her own age.

Marco couldn't concentrate. Was there possibly some way he could stay over there long enough to learn what he wanted to know? He wasn't sure if he wanted that anymore, if it meant what the creatures—and now Lilly—had told him: confronting the naked singularity head-on. He was brave, he was adventurous. But that thing was too much. It made him queasy just to think about it.

"What's with you today, Marco?" his friend Nat asked him at lunch. "What's with this staring off into space? You sick or something?"

Nat lived in the big old house on the hill, not too far from Marco's, in their same neighborhood. They had known each other since they were little. If Marco could tell anyone else about the creatures and the naked singularity, it was Nat. But he couldn't. This was his secret with Lilly, and really, it was too strange to be believed.

"Oh, just family stuff, getting on my nerves," he said.

"Hey, I got an idea," Nat said. "Mom and Dad and I are going on a ski trip this weekend; it's the long three-day weekend, you know? We're leaving right after school to avoid the traffic. You want to come with us? It would be more fun if you were there, and good for you too."

Marco let himself pretend he could go. The ski trip sounded so safe. Last week it would have thrilled him.

"Nat, I can't . . ." But maybe he could tell his *parents* he was going. . . .

He remembered that Nat's family hid a door key in a small wooden outbuilding next to the house—Nat often forgot his key, so they always made sure to leave one there.

A plan was forming in Marco's mind. He was afraid he had an idea that might work.

"Thanks anyway, Nat," Marco said as they started inside. "I have to—to help around the house. I'd love to go another time, though."

If Marco had been a different kind of person, he might not have wanted to walk to and from school with Lilly, whom everyone considered to be so weird. But he didn't care about things like that. And on the way home he told her what Nat had said.

"If Mom and Dad thought I was going skiing with Nat, that would give me from Friday night until Monday night—three days. Not that much time, but better than nothing."

Lilly seemed excited, more hopeful now. "And maybe there's some way we could stretch it, make it more than three days," she said. "I have a feeling there's something I could do."

Marco thought a lot during dinner. Afterward he asked Lilly, "In your dream, they told you they needed you to be a medium between them and . . . the singularity. Do they always need a medium? I mean, why don't they already have one? Is that why they made the tunnel visible to you? Because they needed a new medium now?"

She nodded. "That was one of the first things I asked them, now that you remind me of it. They really didn't want me to know about the last human medium they had, but I said I wouldn't help them unless they told me *something*. So they showed me."

"What?"

"Not much. A woman sitting on a red-and-blue carpet, with a funny box in front of her. And she looked—familiar, somehow. Like I'd seen her in an old photo or something. I still don't understand it. She was smiling in such a strange way."

Now Marco was puzzled that Lilly, who was usually so perceptive, hadn't made the connection. Whom would she have recognized from an old photo? Who had disappeared unexplainably? And who knew things like Lilly did?

Aunt Martha. Had *she* been the previous medium? It made sense that it would run in the family. And what had happened to her?

But Marco didn't want to tell Lilly what he was guessing. If Aunt Martha really had been the previous medium, and then never came back, Lilly would be even more scared.

"But where was it, exactly? Is there any way we can find her and ask her what happened?"

She shook her head hopelessly. "I don't know. I wondered all the same things myself."

"I wonder why they didn't tell you what happened to the last medium," Marco said. "I mean—just how dangerous is it, anyway?"

"I think it's pretty dangerous," she said. "I think that's why they didn't want me to know more."

Marco gulped. If he was the one going over there, then he would be the one who might never come back.

Lilly seemed to sense how worried he was. She touched his hand. "You can do it, Marco," she said, as if she believed it. "I know you—maybe better than you think. And I bet we can work it that you can stay for more than three days too. Tell Mom and Dad you're staying at Nat's house after you come back from the ski trip, to work on some school project. We can get two more days that way, making it five days in all. I'll forge a note from Mom that you're sick or something. I can deal with the school administration."

But not the kids, Marco thought.

Five days was a long time for him to be away from home. But it still wouldn't be very much time in the slow world. He would have to hurry when he was there, and that would make everything more dangerous.

On Friday afternoon, trying not to think too hard about what he was in for, he packed a small suitcase—so his parents would think he was really going on a ski trip—and went to Nat's house.

He wore his backpack, as always.

CHAPTER NINE

Marco walked over to Nat's after school on Friday—he would sneak back to the basement later. Nat's house was at the top of a steep hill, slow going on the icy sidewalk. A gravel driveway went through a gate in a wrought-iron fence and curved slightly as it continued to climb inside their steep property. A short, bumpy lawn sloped up to the house. A couple of tall, thin cypress trees stood beside the drive, and a few other large trees took up most of the lawn.

Marco went to the falling-down outbuilding and pushed

open the door. If the key wasn't where it had been before, he was sunk.

The key was just inside, under a mat. He was relieved to find it—and also scared. Now he really had to do this.

Marco didn't take his coat off inside—it must be more expensive to heat this house than their own, and of course they had turned off the heat anyway.

He had to hide his suitcase so they wouldn't see it during the two days he would be away after they came back. He didn't feel like dealing with another basement. He went up two flights of stairs to the attic.

It was clear that Nat's family rarely if ever came up to the attic. Cobwebs were everywhere, even on the floor; the garment bags hanging on a rack under the eaves were so heavily coated with dust Marco could have written his name on them with his finger.

The roofline was complicated because of the various eaves and turrets. In one dark corner of the attic a short wooden stairway curved up to a closed door. Some of the treads were missing. Marco went carefully up the stairs, and with a lot of effort pushed open the door at the top, loosening dust and bits of plaster.

The room was the top of a small, round turret. There were three windowpanes, at angles to each other, a bay protruding out of the turret. Marco set his suitcase on the floor. He was pretty sure they'd never find it here. And he would come back Wednesday afternoon, when Nat was still at school and his parents were at work, and pick it up before going back home.

Now he had to wait until he was sure his parents were in bed and it would be safe to sneak down to the basement. He went down to Nat's room and found the book on black holes. It was the book where he had first seen the picture of the naked singularity—the more he knew about them, the better. He sat and read, huddled under the blankets on Nat's bed.

These singularities were much more peculiar than ordinary black holes. If the singularity was spinning, an object could get close to it without necessarily being pulled inside and crushed. In fact, the spinning ones spewed things out as well as sucking them in—though more often than not they would spew the object out into another universe. If they really existed, the writer speculated that they might actually be considered to exhibit something like intelligent behavior—and if people ever ran across one, they might think of it as a kind of deity.

That made him think of something, but suddenly he was too hungry to try to figure out what it was. One thing he had forgotten to think about was food. He didn't know if he would be able to eat in the other world. He got out of bed and went down to the kitchen. Luckily there was a big leftover ham in their fridge, and some bread, and he ate as much as he dared.

It was unfortunate that he was going to have to get back into his house through the back door—there was no doorway that went directly to the basement. His parents would have to be deeply asleep not to hear him coming in, so he had to wait. He figured he might as well try to sleep now so he wouldn't have to waste time sleeping in the other world.

Upstairs, he lay down on Nat's bed again and set the alarm for 10:45 P.M. He calculated as he lay there. It was Friday night. He would probably go through at around 11:00 P.M., and come back during the day on Wednesday. That was just about four and a half days of normal time, which converted to only five hours and around ten minutes in the slow world. Not much time. Not much time to face the singularity, and whatever else he had to do.

But that was all the time he would have.

Somehow he was able to fall asleep, and didn't wake up until 10:00 P.M. Only four hours of sleep, but better than nothing.

At 10:45 he carefully locked Nat's door, put the key back in the shed, and started home in the dark and cold. His heart was thudding when he reached his own back door. He carefully slipped the key in the lock, waiting a moment, then softly clicked it open. Holding his breath, he gently pulled the door open and stepped inside. Then he waited.

Darkness and silence. He waited a moment longer, then very, very slowly pushed the door shut and locked it. He tiptoed through the kitchen toward the doorway to the basement.

Upstairs Ruth suddenly howled, "I want a glass of water!" loud enough to wake up everybody in the house. He heard footsteps.

Quickly Marco felt his way down the basement stairs, his hand on the railing. When he reached the root cellar he turned on the light—he needed to see the tunnel entrance, and nobody would notice this light down here, even with Ruth predictably making a fuss upstairs.

And when he turned on the light he saw Lilly waiting there. She had been sitting alone in the dark, and she looked very pale.

And *she* was supposed to help *him*? "How are we going to communicate when I'm over there?" he said. "I can't hear your thoughts. Even if I could, when I'm over there they'll be much too fast to understand."

She shook her head. "I don't know," she said, her voice unsteady. "All I know is they said I could help you. Maybe I'll dream, maybe I'll know what's happening. We just have to try it . . . and hope."

He looked down at Lilly. He thought of Aunt Martha. If he didn't do this, then the burden would all be on Lilly. The *only* way to help her was to go so she could play her part from here.

And he knew he had to hurry. They had said it was already nearly too late over there. He took ten deep breaths, trying to calm his nerves.

"Marco, please come back," Lilly said softly. "Be careful. And . . . good luck."

He didn't turn around to look at her—then he might feel like crying.

He felt Lilly's hand on his leg as he pushed the box through. She seemed reluctant to let go, but did when he crossed the barrier.

CHAPTER TEN

She watched Marco crawl down the tunnel, going slower and slower as he went. Then she waited in the basement for a while after he left, staring at the lights going into the wall. But since she couldn't see what was happening to Marco, what good would it do for her to stay here for hours, like the last time? If she was going to help him, it would have to be through her mind anyway. She might as well go upstairs.

Maybe she would have another dream. The ones before had been vivid, and easy to understand. If the creatures wanted her to help, and they had the capability of communicating with her that way, then she could only hope that they would use that capability again whenever necessary.

But she didn't sleep for a long time. It was Friday night and Marco would not be back until Wednesday—if all went well. Would he be able to stop that terrible thing from coming through? He was brave, and he was adventurous. But he didn't understand and see things the way she did.

Eventually she did fall asleep.

This time the dream was not so clear—but it was much more urgent. The dream was abstract shapes, which made it all the more terrifying. There was a sense of great power, great force, and great danger—danger to Marco.

Marco was going to die—that's all she knew. And nobody was helping him!

She didn't stop to wonder if this was really happening, or just a weird dream. Why weren't the creatures doing anything to help him? *Help him! Hold on to him!* she commanded with all the strength in her mind—and also as slowly as she possibly could, in this emergency situation.

And then she didn't know what happened because she was awake, and she was screaming, "Help him! Hold on to him! Help him!"

Her mother ran into the room and knelt beside her bed, her hand on Lilly's forehead. "What's the matter, darling?

Don't be afraid. It was only a dream. I heard you talking in your sleep the other night too. Is something worrying you?"

What was worrying her was whether Marco had died or been saved. She didn't know—she had woken up before it had happened. She glanced over at the bedside clock. It was after 7:00 A.M.

"I'm . . . I'm okay," she told her mother. "I'm fine. Just a bad dream."

Her mother frowned unhappily. "Well, *I'm* worried. I don't like these sleep problems you're having more and more. I'm going to talk to Dr. Goldman about it. And you must talk with her about it next time. Do you want anything, darling?"

Now Ruth was in the doorway. "I want a drink of water!" she demanded.

Her mother sighed. "Can you please wait just a minute, Ruth? You're not the only child in this family." She turned back to Lilly. "Are you all right now? Do you need anything?"

"I'm fine, Mom," Lilly said, trying to sound convincing.

"Okay, darling. Just remember, we're here for you. You are perfectly safe. Everything's fine." Her mother started to get up.

"It's because she spends so much time down there in the basement," Ruth said.

Lilly wanted to gag her.

"The basement?" said her mother, returning to kneel next to Lilly. "What's this about?"

"Nothing. I like the root cellar. I like it because . . . it makes me think of olden times."

Her mother gave her a strange look, but then smoothed her hair before getting up slowly and moving to the door. "Come on, Ruth," she said rather sharply. "I'll get you your water—again."

Well, at least she *had* been able to try to communicate, to help Marco. Whether it had done anything or not, she didn't know. But she was slightly less scared now.

She just hoped her dreams would happen at such convenient times in the future. But they easily could not.

What would happen if he needed her in some crisis and it was the middle of the day here?

CHAPTER ☀ELEVEN

It was night over here now. Just his luck! And judging by how long the day had gone on—many days back at home—it would be night the whole time he was here. He watched the slow world gradually speed up as his body adjusted to the difference, the creatures moving faster, the swing beginning to fall.

He looked at his watch. It was 11:01. He had until 4:10, to be on the safe side about getting back on time.

In the distance the singularity sparked and crackled. He was going to have to go there. Soon. How big was it, anyway? It was very hard to tell. He could only see part of it.

Here, in the town square, all was bright flickering lights and busy activity and music from a band under a pavilion.

He felt the whoosh of air as he approached the swing, going higher than ever. Why did the creatures believe that this ceremony, this dangerous ritual, would do anything to protect them from the singularity?

When the first creature became aware of him, its head moving back and forth, it stopped and bowed. Then they all did. The swing began to slow down. That was a relief— he thought at first.

A carnival was going on here. Stalls around the old crumbling buildings were selling all kinds of weird food, and oddly shaped black trinkets. The place seemed more crowded, now that night had fallen. Yet the creatures all stopped what they were doing to bow to him and ask him if he had eaten. He did the same thing.

Then, *You say you don't have much time. So hurry, climb on,* came their instructions.

Climb on what? he asked, feeling the beginnings of dread. *I have questions to ask. How is Lilly going to help me, from over there?*

We don't know. Always before it was the medium who came through. This situation is new for us too. Hurry and climb on! they ordered him again.

He turned and looked behind him. There sat half the cardboard box in the alley. Every other time he had been here for only a few minutes. Would the box stay where it was for five hours?

That box, he told them, pointing back at it. *It must not be moved. It is the only way I can find my way back. And I have to go back in five hours—at the very latest.*

It will not be moved, they assured him. *Always before the mediums had something like that to show them the way. But . . . only five hours? That may be a problem.*

Well, it's all the time I have!

Then climb on now! No delay. You must try to take the bag.

And then, finally, he understood. They *had* said it before. He was going to have to ride the giant swing himself, and be the one to grab for the bag—the one who could so easily fall.

Now? he asked them.

The only way for you to appease The Unknowable is to get what the bag contains, they told him.

He didn't know which was worse, the swing or the singularity. But at least the swing was understandable. If he could do that—and live—then he might have more confidence for the next step. And whatever the bag contained, it was clear that it was meant to help him.

Already the front creature had scampered quickly out of the swing and climbed down the ladder leaning against it— even at rest, the swing was too high to get into without the ladder, Marco now saw. The creature was probably *very* relieved that Marco was taking its place. Would he be able to grab the bag? He was small, but the adult creatures weren't any bigger than he was. And their front limbs were shorter than his arms. Maybe it would be easier for him, he tried to tell himself.

Wondering if he would ever get back home, he put his hands on the ladder. It was at least twelve feet high. He had grown stronger and hardly felt the pull of the extra gravity as he climbed, two of the creatures steadying the ladder. Marco did not look down—he had never climbed this high on a ladder back at home. He hated heights. When at last he reached the top, panting already, he stepped carefully down into the boat-shaped swing. It had seats like a rowboat, and wooden handholds to grab onto to push and pull to make it swing. It creaked before it even started to move.

The ladder was carried away. Two groups of creatures pulled on ropes attached to the front and back of the swing to get it started. The creatures in the swing with Marco swayed back and forth. As the swing gained momentum, the creaking got louder. The creatures on the ground dropped the ropes.

Don't just sit there! You must help too. Otherwise we will never get high enough.

Marco began to rock in rhythm with the others. The swing rose and fell. Every time it swept down, Marco felt his stomach rise up, sickeningly. He had never liked amusement park rides, or even normal swings, for that matter. He was glad he hadn't eaten much that day.

Everyone on the swing faced in the same direction. As the swing rose higher, Marco could see more and more of this world that he had only rushed in and out of before. This was a village of low grayish buildings, and the swing rose above all in the central square. There was hardly anybody wandering the streets. Almost the entire population seemed to be at this ceremony.

Some of the houses were richer and fancier than the others, and had high gates around their gardens. So there *were* gardens after all. Lilly had not been entirely wrong, about the gardens as well as the rich houses. There was even a strange building with a sharply pointed roof that might be the temple she had mentioned. But there were no bright colors, only the same dull gray.

The swing fell, and rose again, higher.

He also could tell now that there were good and bad viewing spots for the giant swing ceremony. In the best ones, closest to the swing, in a kind of bleacher, sat sleek and plump creatures. The ones that were crowded together precariously on little balconies were not so plump and sleek, and their hides were more mottled. Clearly there were rich and poor here. And the poor seemed to be underfed, and less healthy.

He took one quick glance backward at the two other swing riders behind him. They were not plump and sleek. It was the poor who were forced to risk their lives on this thing—the poor, and Marco.

Higher and higher, rocking, the little cloth bag growing closer now. For the first time Marco noticed a faint glow coming from the small pouch. Soon it would be close enough for him to reach for it. Would he even have the nerve to try? He still didn't know.

He was sweating heavily, grunting with the effort, pushing as hard as he could to get the swing high in the air. The higher they were, the closer he would be to the bag, and the less likely to fall.

He glanced up, past the cloth bag, and for the first time noticed that there were two moons, one small and bluish and near the horizon, the other one large and orangy, in the center of the sky. The swing was high enough now for him to see more of the landscape outside the village, illuminated by the double moonlight. Mostly it was just a flat, grassy plain, with occasional tall, gnarly trees.

The one striking feature, of course, was the plateau in the distance—the plateau from which the singularity warped and seethed, shooting off sparks, the fiery mass bright enough to leave an impression when he closed his eyes against it. He hated heights, but he hated that thing more.

Go on! We are high enough. Reach for it now. Then our

team will win! And then you . . . The rest of the thought remained hidden from him.

The swing swooped from near the ground up to a point where its supporting cables were just a little above the horizontal. Marco held his breath and stretched forward, reaching. His hand was a good two inches from the bag. The swing dropped down and zoomed up the other way.

Push harder! Push harder! the creatures exhorted him and themselves. And to him they complained, *Stretch farther! You have long front limbs. Do not think about falling.*

Easy for them to say! Up flew the swing. Marco stood up and leaned out over the front edge of the boat, which was at such a high angle that he seemed to be standing upright even though he was tilting forward. The boat railing was very low; it felt as though almost nothing was keeping him inside now. He teetered, he slipped and almost fell. And he missed the bag by an inch.

Plummeting down again, slipping back into the boat, rocking, the wind whistling past, vaguely aware of the screaming crowd. Up the other way. Down. And up toward the bag.

He stretched. He was grasping the railing with one sweaty hand. But this time he realized that he couldn't stretch far enough if he held on. He had to risk letting go. He reached out with both hands as the swing approached the top of its arc.

There was the bag, so close, so close! Maybe he was going to get it.

But he was about to fall. A burning fear raced through him, balance gone, beginning to topple.

Help him! Hold on to him! ordered another, utterly distinct voice inside his head. It was distinct because it was so quick and high-pitched that it was like a tape played too fast. And yet—inexplicably—he could understand it.

Pincers grabbed at his feet. The creature behind him had heard the voice too. It was saving him! He stretched just that much farther and grabbed the bag. And before he fell to the ground far below, the creature behind him pulled him back into the boat.

He had beaten gravity. And now a great cheer went up from the crowd as all the creatures in the swing stopped pumping. *Thank you! Oh, thank you for saving me!* Marco mentally cried to the creature behind him, turning to look at it, almost wanting to hug it.

But he knew whose fast little voice had really saved him. It was Lilly.

CHAPTER TWELVE

In the town square all was jubilation.

One creature carried Marco on its back and the others paraded around the giant swing behind them, cheering and shouting. Marco had never played football but he imagined that this was how someone would feel after making a winning touchdown. And he loved it.

A part of his brain tried to remind him that he wasn't really the hero. Lilly was—without her, he never would have gotten the prize. *But I'm the one who took the risk*, he argued with himself.

And he would be dealing with the singularity next.

But Lilly doesn't know anything about singularities, he thought. *He* was the one who had read all about them. He would be in charge.

And that made him remember the bag. He was still clutching it. It was heavy for its size, a cloth bag, fastened at the top with a complicated knot. Was it his to keep? They had said it was the first thing he needed—to face the singularity, and to learn how to go everywhere there was to go. They had also said something about a holy relic, whatever that was.

Finally, they put him down, and bowed to him again. *You have completed the first step toward appeasing The Unknowable. We must eat and drink! We must all feast in celebration!*

That made him think of the time. He quickly looked at his watch. It was 11:23. A precious twenty minutes had gone by. He had only four hours and fifty minutes left.

I have less than five hours before I have to go back. I don't have time for a feast. He also wasn't sure he would be able to eat their food—they looked so different, their metabolisms were probably a lot different too. And he noticed, now that he had more time, that there were powerful rotten fishy smells wafting through the air. *Can I . . . open the bag?* he asked them. *And what do I do with whatever is inside?*

Yes! Open the bag. You have won it. Open it and see! If

you persist in believing that you have only five more hours here, then you must act at once! He could tell they were slightly offended, probably because he had refused their invitation to eat—eating must be like a ritual, if it was part of their normal greeting. But he couldn't help it. He had to get back.

Carefully he undid the complicated knot. Inside the bag was a metal box, very plain and old-looking, stained and a little dented. He frowned. *This is it?* he asked them.

Why do we detect a tone of disappointment in your thoughts? You do not think it is good enough for you?

Well, I did risk my life for it, he pointed out. *Can you tell me what it is, please, and how I'm supposed to use it?*

First you must go to The Unknowable with it—it can only be activated there. And if you succeed with it, and appease The Unknowable—and also happen to survive—then you will be able to go everywhere there is to go.

He didn't want to say it, but he knew time was passing. *Then I really don't have time for feasting and celebration. I've got to keep going with this so I can get back in time. Because if I don't get back in time, I'll be in really big trouble.*

Laughter.

Trouble? We can see in your mind that the trouble you will be facing in your world is nothing *compared to the absolute disaster we will all face if you do not succeed here.*

And then their thoughts went dead—absolutely dead. He assumed that they were conferring together in secret, discussing things they did not want him to hear. Their honoring him for winning the giant swing ritual had been brief indeed.

They came back suddenly. *Most of us will stay and eat, because we want to, and because it is the proper thing to do. Some will go with you to transport you to The Unknowable. It is a journey of approximately one of your hours.*

An hour? He was horrified. *That means two whole hours are going to be eaten up just getting there and back. That leaves me less than three to do whatever I have to do.*

An hour it must be. Be grateful that you do not have to walk.

Two of the mangier-looking creatures hurried over to him. Each was carrying two wooden poles, upon which rested a chair, one creature in the front and one in the back. They were going to carry him in this ancient contraption?

You don't have cars, automobiles, horses, anything faster than this? Marco asked them. He didn't like the idea of these two creatures having to carry him, even though he wasn't very heavy.

Their tone was insulted. *What is wrong with the chair? It is one of the best ones we have, in your honor.*

But why don't I just walk, then, instead of making people carry me?

They will go faster than you would go on foot. They are used to the gravity. You will see. They will give you instructions too. And since you have so little time—please be on your way.

And in a moment they were. The creatures *did* go faster than he would have, hurrying along on their four hind limbs. But he still didn't like it that they were the poor, less healthy-looking ones. It seemed unfair that they should be burdened with him.

Out of habit, he put the box he had won in his backpack. But it pressed uncomfortably into his spine when he leaned against the seat, so he took it out and put it down beside him.

Soon the village, with its lights, was behind them. The smaller of the two moons had set, but there was enough light from the other one to see the raised dirt pathway that ran between the rectangular marshy fields. The chair was not built for a human boy; the chair back was too low and the seat was too long. The ride was also bumpy. Still—especially after what he had been through on the giant swing—Marco was glad he was not walking.

But he felt bad about the ones who were carrying him. *Is this your job?* he asked them. *It seems like hard work. And you don't look . . . er, as healthy as some of the other ones.*

They are the rich. They are fatter, but we are stronger than they are. They do not do work like this. This is our place. There was no complaint in their tone.

But there was fear about where they were going. Marco looked ahead at the glowing, spitting mass of the singularity. How close were they going to have to get to that thing?

So, there are rich and poor in your society, and no one in between? he asked them. He was curious, but he was also avoiding the main issue. He knew he was going to have to ask them about the singularity before they got there, but he wanted a little respite first.

There are rich and there are poor. That is the way. The rich deal with the important issues. We keep things running.

And it's the poor who have to risk their lives on the giant swing too, right? he asked them.

Of course. That is the way. They didn't sound quite so accepting of it now.

Marco thought of something else. *If you are not of the richer classes, then, and not used to doing the important things, will you be able to help me to know how to deal with the singu—I mean with The Unknowable?*

They did not answer immediately, trotting along. *Of course, they chose us to go because it is very dangerous. But all of us know as much as anyone can about The Unknowable—The Lord. We live so close to It that It has been the most important part of our lives and culture throughout our entire history. We have almost been destroyed by It, and have finally learned how to try to prevent the calamity, with the help of the master box. You will have instruction . . . and it is possible that It might even help you.*

"Gee, that's encouraging," he muttered aloud. What was he getting into? Did he really have to do this at all? It was only their word.

And Lilly's. Lilly he trusted. But what she knew about this was also what she had heard from them. Maybe he was putting himself in danger just by offering to help *them*— and if he didn't do any of this, nothing bad would happen in his own world at all. Maybe he should just turn around and go back.

He was making excuses. He knew what he had read in real scientific books about naked singularities and the fiery chain reactions that ripped through the wormholes they created, causing the end of many universes. He couldn't go back.

They had reached the bottom of the plateau now. The ground was rising, the path turning in switchbacks. Naturally the creatures were going slower and breathing more heavily.

Now Marco noticed something very strange. The seat he was sitting in was sinking, sagging, creaking under his weight. It hadn't done that before.

Is my seat breaking? he asked them. *What's going on?*

Their breathing was so labored now that if they had to communicate verbally, they probably wouldn't have been able to. *We are getting closer to The Lord. Things change as you approach. Look back, look back at the village.*

They were high enough now, almost to the top of the low plateau, so that he had a good view of the countryside in the bright orange moonlight. He turned and looked back at the village, which he could see very clearly.

And his heart almost stopped.

The giant swing was a blur. The creatures bustling around it were blurs. The village had speeded up tremendously.

His chair sagged even more as they reached the top of the plateau. The creatures carrying him were gasping.

Of course. It made complete sense, he realized as a terrible fear clutched at his gut. They were a lot closer to the singularity now. Gravity was stronger here. And that inevitably meant time was slower.

He looked at his watch. It was only just after midnight. And maybe they would reach the singularity in an hour, his time.

But back in the village, many hours were going by. They had purposely misled him. Because if many hours were going by in the village, then many *days* were going by back at home, where time was so much faster.

He would never get back in time. It was probably *already* past the time for him to be back home. They might be missing him right now.

He was trapped in a deep, deep time well.

And then he noticed something funny about the shadows of the slowly plodding bearers and his chair on the flat ground. Why were the shadows stretching out like that?

He looked up, actually groaning aloud with fear now.

The big orange moon was visibly sliding across the sky.

CHAPTER THIRTEEN

Lilly's appointments with Dr. Goldman were after school on Wednesdays. She hated them. At school she could fade anonymously into the background, most of the time. But in Dr. Goldman's office, the attention was all focused on her.

"Your mother tells me you've been having bad dreams," Dr. Goldman said, leaning forward athletically from behind her desk. "Can you tell me about them?"

Of course she couldn't tell her about the tunnel, and the slow world, where Marco was, and how she had forged the note to the school from her mother that Marco was sick.

Thank heaven he would be back home today! But first she had to get through the next thirty minutes.

The dream she had had last Friday night was so vague and abstract that she could probably just tell the doctor about it without giving anything away. She was still worried because the dream had not indicated what had happened, whether Marco had lived or not. She could only hope that she had helped him, as the creatures had promised her she could. She would find out when she got home today and saw Marco.

But now she had to deal with Dr. Goldman. "Well, er, the last dream was really vague," she said. "It's like I didn't really know where I was or anything. I just knew that Marco was in danger, that he was going to die—and that there was somebody there that could help him if they knew. So I was trying to tell them to help him. And that's what I was saying when I woke up, and Mom heard me."

Dr. Goldman sat back in her chair, crossing her trim legs and shaking back her stylish brown hair. "So you were scared of something happening to Marco. I know how important he is to you, Lilly. But you know, you can't go on depending on your older brother for everything. You need friends your own age, girlfriends . . ."

And she was off on that old riff again. Lilly hardly had to listen, making routine answers when the doctor urged her to be more friendly with other girls at school, asking her the names of the ones she talked to, on and on. She could handle this automatically while worrying about Marco, impatient to see him and find out what had happened.

". . . the basement," she noticed Dr. Goldman was saying. "What's this your mother told me about spending a lot of time down there?"

"I like the basement," Lilly said defensively. "I like the root cellar because I like to think about the days when people stored their vegetables there, before they had fridges. I like old things. It's like . . . going back in time, or something."

"But why don't you want Ruth to go down there?" she asked Lilly, just noticeably frowning a little. "Why did you tell her that awful story about a little girl disappearing? That wasn't a very nice thing to do to a seven-year-old."

So Ruth had told that story to Mom, despite swearing she would not. Lilly should have known she would. She also felt a pang of guilt for telling Ruth such a scary story. What could she say to get out of this one?

"Er . . . Dr. Goldman, I don't think you know Ruth very well. Maybe Mom didn't tell you what she's like. She's real snoopy, and she wants attention all the time. Sometimes I want her to leave me alone. And she's tough too. A story like that isn't going to . . . I don't know the word . . . it's not going to make her crazy or anything like that. It will just keep her out of the basement so I can have some time alone there."

"Well, she does sound quite different from you, if she wants attention all the time." Dr. Goldman was studying Lilly with her hands pressed together. "I think it would be better to just ask her politely to go play by herself, instead of making up frightening stories."

"Okay, I'll do that. I promise," Lilly said quickly. "And the dreams aren't so bad. Mom just worries."

Dr. Goldman sighed. "Well, I'm afraid time's up," she said. "See you next week. I think we did accomplish something today."

That was what she always said at the end of the appointments.

Lilly was impatient in the car on the way home. It was almost five. Marco would have to be home when she got there.

But he wasn't waiting for her in the living room. He wasn't in his own room. And he wasn't in the basement.

Was it possible he hadn't come back from the slow world yet? But he knew he could only get away with missing two days of school. Had something happened to him there? Had he died after all, and she *hadn't* saved him?

Maybe he had come home and then gone out again. "You seen Marco at all?" she asked Ruth in the kitchen, as casually as she could.

"No. Why? Isn't he home yet?" Ruth said.

Their mother was cooking supper. "That *is* strange," she said. "He was supposed to come back from Nat's after school today. I'll just give them a call and find out what's going on."

"No. Don't do that!" Lilly said, without thinking.

"Why on earth not?" her mother said suspiciously. "Lilly. Is there something you're not telling us?"

"No. No, er, nothing," Lilly said, at a complete loss.

"Well, I'm calling," her mother said. And then she found out that Marco hadn't been on the ski trip at all. Their father came home as she was slowly hanging up the phone.

"It's too late to call the school," her mother said, her face pale. "But he wasn't with Nat's family all weekend. What do you know about this, Lilly? You and Marco are so tight. Why didn't you want me to call Nat's?"

Lilly had never been in such a tough spot in her life. And if Marco didn't come home soon, it would get worse and worse. "I . . . I don't know why I said that," Lilly said lamely. "I mean, you know how Marco is. He loves to explore. He's always taking long rides on buses and commuter trains. I thought maybe he just took a longer trip or something, and didn't want anybody to know."

Her parents looked at each other, very worried now. "Buses and trains? Since when?" her father said.

"He's been doing it since he was really young, like Ruth's

age," she said. "He didn't want anybody but me to know about it. I'm sure he's okay. He just took a trip or something. . . ."

But of course she wasn't sure he was okay. Maybe he was already dead. Anything could happen to him over there. She began to cry, she just couldn't help it.

Her mother found the number of Marco's homeroom teacher and called her at her house. Now they knew he had not been at school since last Friday—and today was Wednesday. They called the police.

She thought Dr. Goldman was bad! The police quizzed her, and they weren't real gentle about it. Everybody was sure she knew something she wasn't telling.

She kept hoping that Marco would come up the basement stairs, just delayed for a few hours—that could happen so easily, where nine minutes there would add up to several hours here.

And every minute, Marco did not show up.

They asked her if she had forged the note to the school. She denied it. She denied everything. "Marco has friends. He has friends I don't even know. They could have written the note," she said tearfully. "Don't you think I'm scared too? Don't you think I'm worried about him?"

She was even thinking that maybe she should tell them about the tunnel. But somehow she knew that would not work, with the police and her parents. They probably would not be able to go through, and anyway, she didn't *want* them to go through. If she told them, they would just think she was crazier than they already thought she was. And the more she thought about that, the more she began to see what the only solution was, if Marco did not show up by late that night.

She would have to go through by herself.

She did tell them that Marco traveled widely. That was only going to make the pointless police search more difficult.

The atmosphere in the house was grim when the police finally left. There was no dinner; they just nibbled. Her parents were still suspicious of her, she felt it. She went to bed as early as she reasonably could.

And at midnight, when her parents had finally gone to bed, she snuck down to the basement. She never could have done this—alone!—if she hadn't been so worried about Marco. But for Marco she could do anything.

She crawled into the tunnel.

CHAPTER ☀FOURTEEN

The first thing she came across was the box Marco had left halfway into the tunnel. She left it where it was and crawled forward.

And then her arms almost buckled under her, she felt so heavy. She stayed on her hands and knees, looking at the slow world.

And it was not the way they had shown it to her in her dreams. It was like Marco had said—drab, colorless old buildings and dust, no gardens and golden palaces and banners and streamers. She looked at the swing hanging so high, and the creatures barely moving. It was terrifying.

She gritted her teeth and crawled a little farther, around the box. The world began to speed up—though she knew what was really happening was that she was slowing down.

And then they sensed her presence. She stayed kneeling by the box, feeling too weak even to be able to stand in this gravity, as they rushed toward her, bowing and bowing, their heads moving strangely back and forth. At least they were the same as she had seen in her dream. And they needed her so much! That made it a little less frightening.

First they asked her if she had eaten yet, which she didn't understand, but just said she had. Then they said, *Oh, thank you for coming! We are so happy to see you, Lilly. Come in, stay, and eat.*

I can't stay. You don't understand. We are only children. I am eleven years old. They're already going crazy because Marco has been missing for so long. I can't disappear too. Just tell me—is Marco okay? I want to see him. Is he safe? Where is he?

You saved him on the giant swing. Now he is making the pilgrimage to The Unknowable. He has not reached it yet.

Relief flooded through her. *Then he's still alive? He's safe?*

Yes, he is alive. Whether he is safe or not we will not know until he reaches The Unknowable. It will take him many more days.

Many more of your days? she asked them, horrified.

Yes. The closer he gets, the slower he goes. And when he arrives, you will have to help him. Stay here! It will be easier for you to help him from here.

She dared now to look up into the distance, to the thing they had never shown her. It was just as awful as Marco had said, and she quickly looked away from it. *Why did you show me golden buildings and gardens and temples? Why didn't you ever show me The Unknowable?* she asked them. *You lied to me.* She dared to be like this because she was so afraid for Marco.

We do not lie. We showed you what our perceptions are. You do not understand. We do not see with light, as you do. We send out signals and they bounce back to us. You would say we are blind. But we can sense things in our own way. And what we showed you is how we sense our world.

So that was why they were always moving their heads in that strange way. They were blind, and they "saw" with something like sonar. And so what they perceived that way was different from what human eyes could see. They made their world more beautiful to themselves.

She had to get back now. She knew Marco was safe, and time was racing by at home, and she could not disappear like he had. *You say I can still help him, from my world?*

Yes, though it will not be as easy. We will send you the messages when he needs you.

Thank you. I must go back now.

They bowed and bowed to her as she turned and crawled with such great difficulty back to the box and around it, and finally, with huge relief, into the basement, and normal gravity.

She just sat there for a moment, sighing deeply with happiness. There were bad problems ahead of her, dealing with everybody about what had happened to Marco. But at least she knew that he was alive, and that she could help him. She would be ready to do anything she could, as soon as they sent her the next dream.

She was twenty years old when it came.

CHAPTER ☼FIFTEEN

The bearers set the chair down to rest as the large hot sun popped over the horizon and sailed up into the sky. Marco wanted to urge them to hurry, but pushed away the thought—they must be exhausted, carrying him in this gravity.

Still, the situation was the nightmare of all nightmares for Marco, who had never been late since that one time when he was seven. There was no doubt that he had already been missing for many, many days back at home.

How on earth was Lilly dealing with this? And his parents? What was Lilly telling them? It was too awful to think about.

You must wear this now. The mediums from your world always need it when they confront The Lord.

One of them took from the bag on its back a piece of black glass, a curving rectangle, with a wooden earpiece on either side of it. Dark glasses. They didn't seem to have plastic here. *You mean, so I can look at it directly without hurting my eyes?* he asked them.

Correct.

But why don't you need to wear them?

You didn't notice yet? And we were beginning to think you were intelligent, for your species. We do not see the way you do. You would think of us as blind. We send out signals and they bounce back to us. That is why we do not "see" The Unknowable as you do.

And that must also be why the pictures they sent to Lilly were so inaccurate, he realized.

Marco fit the contraption over his head. It was large for him, but it would have to do. It did not fall off, at least. Now he could look directly at the sun as it sank down and night fell. The two moons sweeping in complex patterns across the sky were almost invisible to him with the dark glasses on.

The bearers took deep breaths and picked up the chair.

Only a little farther now, they told him. They began plodding toward the singularity again as Marco's chair sank lower and lower toward the ground. The poles seemed to be made of some solid yet flexible plant material.

He looked straight ahead, long and hard at the naked singularity for the first time.

From this vantage point he could see, as he had not seen before, that it was not actually *on* the surface of this planet, it was in fact hanging above the plateau. That made sense. If it had been on the planet, the planet would be torn to shreds by the singularity's immense gravitational tidal forces. It was impossible to tell how far away it was. But they were still close enough to feel the powerful effects of its gravity.

And it was spinning so fast! That meant that if they got too close to it and got sucked inside, they might not be crushed by the gravity, as they would have been had it been an ordinary nonspinning singularity. The spin meant that it was a pathway to other universes, as Nat's physics book had said. Getting pulled into its radius would probably mean being thrown out again into another space and time. And then he might never get home.

They were moving toward an ancient and huge stone archway that from this point framed the singularity. There was a wall all the way along the top of the plateau and across the bottom of the archway, a wall too high to climb, with no breaks, and no steps—only a sloping ramp, directly under the archway. This seemed to be as far as they were going to go.

Perhaps the wall was the boundary, the cutoff point, beyond which anything would be pulled into the singularity. Black holes had what was called an "event horizon," the point at which the gravity became so strong that light could not escape—once you got past it, you were pulled in. You could see the event horizon of a black hole. Since this singularity had no black hole around it, there was no visible event horizon. Perhaps this wall had been built to indicate where this singularity's event horizon would have been.

The singularity itself was a chaotic mess. Sparks of light of all colors sizzled and exploded randomly out of it. Other beams of light spiraled dizzyingly around it as it spun. Some things seemed to be shooting into it too. There was no order to it, no predicting when and where the next particular event would happen.

From here he could also see that it wasn't just light being spewed out of the thing. There were objects too—dust, rocks, even some things that seemed to be artifacts, mechanisms, gadgets, springs—falling from it to the ground. He remembered reading in the book about singularities, what seemed like years ago at Nat's house, that some scientists speculated this is exactly what would happen with a naked singularity: Objects from other universes would be ejected from it.

You could say it was like a cosmic revolving door. An object entered it from one universe, and then could exit into an infinite number of other universes, all connected by the singularity's gravitational distortion of spacetime.

When he brought himself to look away from it for a moment, he could see that there were heaps of these objects on the other side of the wall. Another reason not to go over there, or you'd be brained by them. Yet at the same time some of these objects were also being pulled *into* it. Weirdly, the gravity worked both ways. But the book had said that too. And that such an object might display what appeared to be intelligent behavior, taking some objects and discarding others, as if it were acting with some great purpose.

And on this world, they believed it did, that it was *The Lord*. And so they had invented the giant swing ceremony, thinking to please it.

Marco looked quickly back at the singularity. That was the oddest thing of all—he could hardly bear to look away from it. Whereas before it had been a painful sight that he had cringed from, here he felt a powerful attraction to it. And, despite knowing that time at home was streaking by at an unimaginable rate, he did not want to go away from the thing either.

The sun and the moons were now moving so fast that the distinction between night and day had ceased to be noticeable. The sky around the singularity was a gray blur. Of course this did not mean that the universe had speeded up. It meant that where they were, time was going incredibly slowly, so the rest of the universe was going faster only relative to them.

They stopped at a stone slab near the wall. The bearers set the chair on the slab. From here, Marco could see just over the wall and through the arch.

This is as far as we can go, the bearers told him, awe in their thought patterns. They both fell to the ground, prostrating themselves in front of the thing they called The Lord. Now he could hear their minds chanting something that he could not understand.

Er . . . but what am I supposed to do now? Marco asked them. *I thought you were going to give me instructions.*

Take what you won on the giant swing from its bag.

Marco had forgotten about that worthless-looking old metal box that he had risked his life for, that he would have died for if Lilly hadn't saved him. He reached over to pick it up from where he had set it beside him on the adult-sized chair.

The bag slipped right out of his fingers. It had, of course, grown a lot heavier since he had plucked it from the pole. He tried again, using both hands, and with a great deal of effort was able to lift the bag onto his lap. There he untied the cord, fumbling, and finally dragged the metal box out of it.

Now what do I do? he wanted to know.

He could sense their irritation at being interrupted from their prayers. *The box came from The Lord. It fell on this side of the wall, away from everything else. That is how we know it is one of the special relics. Now that you have won it on the giant swing, you must take it back inside. And once you are there, you must find and bring back the master box, which has been stolen. The master box is our part of The Lord. It tells us The Lord's will. We must have it back.*

Inside? Over the wall? But . . . but that's where things are being sucked into it, he thought back at them.

That is what the other mediums did. And some of them even came back. You are on your own now. We must pray.

Some of them even came back . . . Marco thought. He couldn't deny that he did feel the attraction of this very peculiar astronomical object. It *was* a way to other universes, for sure. What was he going to do? What would happen if he just refused?

Or never came back.

You must go inside or you will never learn how to go everywhere there is to go. And The Lord will quickly become destructive—to our world, and to many of the worlds con-

nected to us, including yours. Why do we have to spell
everything out for you so many times? We must pray.

What was he going to do? Was that all they were going
to tell him?

They had said that Lilly—the true medium—would be
able to help him here, as she had helped him on the giant
swing. But that seemed utterly impossible to him now. At
the giant swing he had only been going twenty-one times
slower than his own world. Here, he was going many *many*
times slower than that. It didn't seem as though there was
any way that Lilly could communicate with him.

And the longer he just sat here, doing nothing, the more
time would be rocketing by back at home. Maybe he didn't
have to actually go over the wall himself. Maybe he could
just drop the little box over, and see what happened.

He inched his way out of the chair and off the stone slab
onto the ground. He could not walk here, he was far too
heavy. He crawled, painfully slowly, pushing the metal box
ahead of him. It would have ripped a hole in his backpack
now if he had tried to carry it that way.

He reached the ramp. Now he could see that there were
ridges in it, like handholds. That was how the other mediums had pulled themselves up. It would have been impossible without them. With all the strength in his body, Marco
dragged himself up the ramp, pushing the heavy little box
ahead of him. He had to keep stopping to rest. He didn't

know if he had the strength to get all the way to the top. But he kept moving, taking it one minute at a time, resting and gasping.

At last he reached the top. He lay there panting for a few minutes, while days rushed by back at home. Then he managed to lift the box to drop it over the edge.

And as soon as his hand crossed the top edge of the ramp, he felt it. The pull of the singularity. Both his arms shot upward; they felt as though they were being stretched out like taffy. He was dragged up the ramp. Up, over to the other side. He screamed. Objects and sparks of light swirled around him. His bones creaked as the part of his body closer to the singularity was stretched even more. A deep rumbling filled his ears, the white noise of the singularity. . . .

The singularity growing larger and larger and more and more volcanic as he fell toward it . . .

The singularity engulfing him . . .

At that moment, they were celebrating Lilly's twentieth birthday.

After high school, Lilly had decided to stay home and help her parents rather than go to college or get her own place. College or an apartment were both too expensive. And she needed to stay close to the tunnel in the basement, to be ready whenever Marco needed her, and to be there when he came back.

She had a friend now, a boy named Carl. He was shy too, and liked science. He was understanding, not asking about

Marco, but listening when she talked about how he might come back one day.

The world had changed when Marco disappeared.

Their parents' hopes had gradually faded over the first few months, and after a year the police had given up their nationwide search for him. It had been terrible for Lilly and for Ruth to see their parents so grim, all the pleasure gone out of their lives. Only after years had Mom and Dad stopped thinking about Marco all the time, and blaming themselves for not watching him closely enough, and not preventing whatever terrible thing had happened to him.

Lilly kept checking the slow world, and they continued to assure her that he was still on his way to The Lord. *The closer he gets, the slower he goes,* they explained to her again, and she tried to make sense out of it. She got science books from the library, hoping to understand about black holes and time and singularities, but her mind did not work the way Marco's did. The things she knew, that nobody else knew, were natural things that happened effortlessly to her—they just came into her mind. Understanding physics was not one of them. After she got to know Carl, she sometimes asked him questions, but his answers didn't help her much either.

Meanwhile, she had to pretend she was as miserable as her parents. She *was* genuinely unhappy, worrying about Marco and missing him, so it was not that hard an act to take it one step further and pretend she was grieving for him. In a way she was, because she knew enough to realize that what he was doing was very dangerous, and he really *might* never come back. It also made her nervous, because she knew that a lot of what happened to him would be determined by her. The creatures had told her that.

Lilly's parents had eventually stopped suspecting she was hiding something, but not Ruth. Ruth was sixteen now, and she wasn't dumb.

Ruth had been only seven when Marco had disappeared, and he had been a rather distant older brother to her, so she was not devastated by loss, as her parents were. What she was, was curious. Not curious enough to go down into the basement alone—as tough as she was, that was the one place that still scared her—but curious enough to keep her eye on Lilly, to listen closely to what Lilly said, and watch what she did when she thought nobody was looking.

Ruth had always craved attention and love from Lilly. Now that she was older, the need was not as strong. But she still couldn't understand why Lilly was so fixated on this phantom older brother, who everybody believed was gone forever. Why didn't Lilly pay more attention to Ruth, who was still around? She couldn't stop wondering about it. And hurting.

She thought about all the things Lilly had inexplicably known, for as far back as she could remember. And Lilly kept on knowing things too.

"Somebody took my favorite knife and didn't put it back in the right place," their mother would complain in the kitchen, pulling open the knife drawer as she fixed a snack for Ruth.

"You left it in the sink," Lilly said, pausing in the kitchen door.

Their mother looked in the sink. "Oh. That's right, I did," she said, and went on with her cooking.

Ruth looked over at Lilly, who didn't meet her eye and hurried away.

Their parents kept Marco's room exactly the way it had been, as though they were still hoping he might come home someday. But the only person who ever went in there was Lilly. Ruth would peek around the edge of the doorway, watching Lilly, frowning in puzzlement. She made sure Lilly didn't know she was watching.

And why was Lilly always reading science books, taking notes as if she were still in school? What was she hoping to find out?

Ruth never went to the basement, but she saw Lilly go down more than anyone else in the family. What was it about the basement? Before Marco's disappearance, he and

Lilly had spent so much time down there. She was sure it had something to do with what had happened to Marco.

Most important of all, Ruth remembered—even though she was only seven at the time—that Lilly had really not been as upset as her parents when Marco disappeared. She seemed to feel *guilty* about something when the police questioned her. And she had not grieved the way their parents had. Mom and Dad were too caught up in their own sadness to notice, but Ruth could see that Lilly was not as unhappy as she would have expected. Lilly and Marco had always been so close that she should have been beside herself when it became clear that he was never coming back. But she wasn't. She was strangely calm about the whole thing.

When Ruth was younger she would have pointed these things out to her parents, but now she was learning to hide information, to keep it secret and save it up, for when it would be the most useful.

Lilly's friend Carl was the only guest at her birthday party. What was peculiar was that Lilly didn't seem to mind that she had only one friend.

Ruth had reached the age at which it is important to be cool and popular. She was plump, but that didn't keep her from having her own circle of friends who loved to gossip and make fun of people who were different. Ruth was proud of being the best at this game, and she was often angered and embarrassed by her strange older sister. But she still loved her, in her limited way. Lilly had been so kind to Ruth for all of her life that despite her own failings, Ruth still wanted to be loved by her. She didn't understand why Lilly couldn't stop thinking about Marco all the time.

Lilly took a deep breath and blew out all twenty candles on her birthday cake. Before Marco disappeared, their mother had made birthday cakes from scratch, but now she always bought cake mixes—cheap ones, of course—and they weren't as good. Ruth loved sweet things.

Everybody clapped, their parents rather halfheartedly, Carl enthusiastically. It was Carl who urged Lilly to make a wish.

Lilly closed her eyes and furrowed her brow for a moment. Ruth would have given almost anything to know what she was wishing for. But she knew you weren't supposed to tell, and though she badgered Lilly about other things, she knew she couldn't get her to reveal her birthday wish.

Lilly cut the cake. She gave Ruth a larger piece than their mother would have done, Ruth was glad to see. Lilly met Ruth's eye when she passed her the plate, which was unusual. It was as though she were saying, *I'm giving you a big piece so please keep your mouth shut about me.* Did Lilly think bribery would work with *her*?

The presents came after they ate the cake. Not a lot of them, and useful rather than lavish—the family still didn't have enough money. Ruth was displeased with their parents about that. She already had her own bank account and was saving up for something special for herself—she wasn't sure what. But it would be something better than the drab sweater and the socks and barrette they gave Lilly.

Carl gave her a book, naturally. His family had more money than Ruth and Lilly's, and it was a lavish astronomy book, big and fat, full of photographs of stars and galaxies, and also drawings of other peculiar objects in space. Lilly seemed thrilled by it.

This was something even their parents were not too out of it to notice. "Really, for someone who never used to have the least interest in science, you're getting very curious about it these days," their mother said.

Lilly just smiled and ducked her head. The party ended when Carl went home.

When Ruth got up in the middle of the night for a secret snack, she saw that Lilly was still up, sitting at her desk, poring over the astronomy book. What was she trying to find? What did she hope to learn?

And most of all, Ruth wondered, did it have something to do with Marco?

Ruth went silently down to the kitchen and had some more cake, wondering about it all.

It was two weeks later, on her way down for another midnight snack, that Ruth heard Lilly talking in her sleep. She stopped in Lilly's doorway to listen.

"Yes . . . Right way . . . Hurry!"

It was hard to understand exactly what Lilly was saying; she was *thinking* more than articulating. But Ruth stood there listening in fascination anyway, and watching closely. Lilly was rolling her head back and forth on the pillow, and she was actually sweating! Clearly she was dreaming about giving directions to somebody—and just as clearly she was terribly afraid. Whatever she was doing was desperately important, in the dream.

"Explore! . . . I want . . . Meant for me . . ."

If it *was* only a dream, that is.

Ruth was not a terribly imaginative person; she was more practical than anyone else in the family. But Lilly had always known things that other people didn't know, and she had known them in some unexplainable way. That could mean that her dreams were more than dreams. Who was she talking to, anyway?

And what would happen if she were interrupted?

"No! . . . Don't . . . Whatever you do . . ." Lilly's thin chest was heaving as she gasped for breath.

Lilly seemed to be suffering. Did Ruth dare to wake her up? In a certain way, the idea was irresistible.

But if it wasn't a dream, and Lilly really *was* guiding somebody, saving somebody—she was behaving as though it was a life-or-death situation—then by waking her, Ruth might be killing whomever Lilly was talking to. Then Ruth would be a murderer. Who would she be murdering?

Could it possibly be Marco? Was he lost somewhere and Lilly was somehow telling him how to get back?

But maybe Ruth didn't want Marco to come back. What had he ever done for her? He had always treated her like she was an irritation, an interruption. Not to mention that, however little money her parents had, there would be less if Marco were around. And Ruth knew that Marco would become the center of their lives, taking away the meager love and attention she received. Lilly and their parents would be so thrilled to have him back! She could hardly stand to picture it.

She took a step into Lilly's room, toward the bed, then stopped and watched her sister.

Ruth tried to convince herself that Lilly couldn't possibly be saving Marco. He had been gone for so long! Anyway, things like that were impossible. It was just coincidence that Lilly seemed to know things. This was nothing but a dream—and a bad one too, from the way Lilly seemed to be suffering and afraid. Ruth would be doing her a favor by waking her up.

Ruth put her hand on Lilly's shoulder and shook it. "Lilly! Wake up! You're having a bad dream!" she said, softly, so her parents wouldn't hear.

Lilly didn't seem to hear her either. She slept on. Then she spoke, but not to Ruth. "Go now . . . No time to lose . . ."

Ruth shook her harder. "Lilly! Wake up!"

"Hurry! . . . Through . . . Then straight ahead and you'll see—"

With both hands Ruth shook Lilly's shoulders up and down. "Lilly! Wake up!"

Then Ruth screamed and jumped backward. Because Lilly didn't just wake up. She started to shake. And the shaking became more violent until she was convulsing on the bed, and drooling, and making choking noises. It was terrifying.

"Mom! Dad!" Ruth shouted, backing away, starting to cry. "Something's happening to Lilly!"

She couldn't bear to watch any more of it. She turned and ran from the room as her parents came rushing in.

No wonder they call it The Unknowable.

The light and falling suddenly stopped, and Marco found himself sprawled in a very strange place, the metal box still in his hand.

The scientists were right about spinning singularities. He wasn't crushed to atoms; he didn't even seem to be hurt. And he wasn't exactly *inside* it.

But wherever he was in its radius, not being crushed meant he was in a place that connected many universes.

And if he went to another universe, would he ever get

home again? He heard the deep rumbling of the singularity's voice. He started to get up.

He couldn't even move, let alone stand, the gravity was so strong. How could he do anything here if he couldn't move? How could he get back to the world he had come from? He wasn't crushed. But was he trapped here by gravity forever?

He couldn't turn his head but he moved his eyes around. What he saw awed and terrified him.

It was the most complicated maze you could imagine, and it went on in all directions. It was like a gigantic expanse of foam. Nothing was solid. All space was punctured by tunnel-like wormholes.

He had no doubt that through the wormholes there were other universes. But he couldn't see through them, let alone *go* through them, since the gravity was so strong he couldn't even lift his head.

A flaming ball of gas shot past him.

Sudden sweat broke out all over his body, his heart pounding. Was this the destructive force of the singularity that the creatures were so afraid of? The destruction that would spread to his world too, zapping it like a meteor, if he did not accomplish what he was supposed to do here?

But how could he do anything if he couldn't move?

He lay there, laboring to breathe, trying not to panic, trying not to let the deepest hopelessness he had ever felt overcome him. And that was when his eyes came to rest on the box, in his hand, just within his field of vision.

The box had changed.

It had no top anymore. Luckily the surface that had vanished was facing him, so he could see inside it. There was a knob, with a dial on it, sort of like a clock with one hand. Only there were no numbers for the dial to point at. Right now the dial was pointing at a strange symbol that looked something like a Chinese character, but different—some alien letter. To the right and left were straight lines. To the left, the lines got wider and wider apart. To the right, they got closer and closer together. What did it mean? Why had it changed within the radius of the singularity? And what would happen if he turned the dial?

But he was sure he was supposed to turn the dial, to use this artifact. That was why he had to win it on the giant swing before coming to the singularity. Was this box what would make it possible for him to do what he had to do here?

He would never know unless he tried.

Another ball of flame shot past him.

With immense effort he was able to move his hand just enough to hold on to the dial. He strained to turn it to the left, where the lines were spaced farther apart.

His hand almost slipped away as he felt it grow heavier. The next ball of flaming gas rocketed past him even faster.

Had turning the knob in that direction made gravity even stronger? Could he hope that turning it the other way would make gravity less?

It took all the strength he had to turn the knob in the other direction. But the more he turned it, the easier it became. He felt himself growing lighter. He could turn his head now. And he could see that the balls of flame were slowing down. He kept turning the knob to the right, the lines growing closer and closer together. And gravity lessened.

If he had felt awe before, it was multiplied many times now. From what kind of universe would a box like this come? Who could have a technology that could control gravity in this way? It was impossible to imagine.

But the fact that he had this box might save his life, his universe, and everything that mattered. The giant swing had been terrifying, but it sure seemed worth it now.

He stopped turning the dial when he was light enough to stand. His heart was pounding again now, not with fear but with pride and excitement. He had never imagined anything so thrilling could happen to him. And now he could move around in the radius of the singularity.

But he still didn't know what he was supposed to do.

Find the right world, Marco. It's not very far.

Lilly! Her voice was much faster than normal, but amazingly he could hear her and understand her. He didn't stop to wonder about how that was possible.

He took a few steps and peered through the closest wormhole that did not look violent. There was another world on the other side. The wormhole opened onto a landscape of turquoise hills. He was amazed to see tall thin people, soaring, rolling, and tumbling through the open space above. It looked like the most fun in the world. And when had he ever had that much fun?

Not that way. Keep going.

He wanted to argue with her, but at the same time he didn't dare to disobey her. He had no clue what universe he was looking for. He turned, avoiding a fiery wormhole, and looked through another calm one. Here there was blackness with a few distant cloudlike clusters of stars. He hurried away, frightened at the possibility of ending up there. The next one contained stairways filling a vast space going in every imaginable direction, up, down, sideways. Little segmented creatures rolled up and down them. The gravity was peculiar: two creatures could be going in the same direction on the same stairway and yet one was going up and the other down.

Not that one either.

He turned away, past an inferno that stung him with heat, and moved toward another one. Here was a vast wasteland, overcast with green haze.

Not there.

Marco moved on. On every side—in front and in back of him, above and below him—were wormholes as far as he could see. Their mouths opened and closed. There seemed to be millions of choices, millions of places to go.

Straight ahead, Marco, Lilly's voice commanded.

Marco walked where she indicated and peered into a wide hole. And he saw a town hanging there, a town that seemed to cover the entire surface of a tiny planet, a beautiful spherical town floating in space.

And he knew that if he went through this wormhole, he would land safely in that town; he knew it as well as he could hear Lilly's voice.

Lovely towers and arcades of golden stone with arched windows, round parks with sculptured fountains. And color! Bright red awnings, blue curtains fluttering in the windows, banners with gorgeous bright designs. There were also darker labyrinthine neighborhoods, begging to be explored. Happy people strolled the wider streets arm in arm, kids laughing, playing games.

People were having more fun there than he had ever experienced. Sure, he had explored the suburbs, and liked it. But he had never, in his whole life, actually had a lot of *fun*. It was irresistible.

Without even thinking, he started through the hole.

Yes, Marco. That's the right way. Go through! Hurry!

*And hide the box. It is very precious. If they know you have
it, they will take it from you.*

Lilly was telling him to do exactly what he wanted to do.
That he didn't mind so much.

But he was irritated with himself for not thinking of hiding the box. He quickly slipped it into his backpack—it was
light enough not to tear it now.

How was he going to get back from this other universe?
How was he going to finish carrying out his mission in the
singularity? He didn't know.

But Lilly was the medium. He was supposed to do what
she said.

He was halfway through the wormhole to the beautiful
town. He ran the rest of the way and plunged out the end.

And found himself in a town square. But oh so different
from the creatures' drab world! The music here wasn't
scratchy and jangling. It jumped and swayed, it made you
want to dance. And people *were* dancing, all around him.

Not people exactly, he saw now. They were humanoid in
shape, but they looked like living jewels. Their smiling
faces reflected the light in dazzling shades of green and red
and blue. Long silver hair drifted slowly behind them as
they threw back their heads and laughed, or gazed at one
another, eyes wide with love.

Dance, Marco, dance! And explore! Lilly was urging him.
I want this dream. Remember, it was meant for me.

Yes, Lilly was the medium, the one who was expected to come here. But he had taken the risk. And he was going to enjoy it, just as she was telling him.

A shimmering girl approached him and opened her arms. Marco had never danced before, but that didn't matter; she swept him away and somehow his legs and feet knew what to do. Spinning, spinning to the glorious music.

And then he saw Lilly, from behind, just leaving the square.

But it couldn't be Lilly! It had to be somebody who just looked like her from the back. Still, he was curious. He smiled at the girl, and bowed, and turned and followed the girl like Lilly out of the arcaded square, past tall brooding towers.

To a long park, with a fountain on the horizon. Across the wide expanse of purple lawn he could actually see the curvature of the planet. The horizon was about as far away from where he stood as the length of a football field.

Gravity should have been almost nothing on a planet this size, only a few miles in circumference, but it felt normal. Perhaps the material of the planet was sufficiently dense to make up the difference. Perhaps it was the box—except that everyone else seemed to be in normal gravity too.

How many millions of light-years were they from Earth?

The girl who looked like Lilly from behind was disappearing over the purple horizon, so fantastically close. He ran after her. And as he ran, the horizon moved ahead of him. He could see the back of her head just above it. He hurried past the splashing fountain.

And now he could see that at the other side of the park was one of the labyrinthine sections of the town. The girl was just running into a narrow alley, shaded from the bright sunlight by a roof of many multicolored umbrellas. He followed her into the dark, narrow, twisting alleyway.

Yes, Marco! This way, this way!

A dark, bearded figure in a long robe leaned out from behind a stall. It held out a sparkling transparent globe filled with intricate mechanisms moving in such complex and unpredictable patterns that Marco did not want to take his eyes away from them. He longed to take it and stare and stare. The figure pointed at Marco's backpack, made a beckoning gesture, and thrust the globe at him.

Could it possibly know he had the precious box in his backpack?

No! Don't let anyone take the box, whatever you do!

He knew that. Why was she even telling him? He could do nothing without this box.

He ran from the figure with the globe, following the girl, who was turning to the right, down an even narrower alley.

Is that you, Lilly? What's happening? I don't understand, he thought at her. They had never read each other's mind before, but anything seemed possible here.

I'll explain everything, if you get home . . . I mean, when you get home. But thank you for coming here so I get to see too.

Past stalls displaying more glowing objects. A little thin four-inch-high clownish figure on a table saluted him and grinned wickedly and suddenly swelled to a fat balloon. On an impulse Marco touched the balloon and it popped, spraying him with bright wriggling confetti, and the clown and the stallkeeper laughed.

The stallkeeper reached for his backpack, more aggressively than the bearded figure had. Marco hurried away. Here was a hooded figure holding in its hand a four-dimensional cube, a real hypercube, a tesseract. He watched in awe as the figure rotated the hypercube, unexpected facets appearing, expanding, contracting. Nothing like this existed on Earth.

But he couldn't pause too long, or someone might get the box. And the girl was always just ahead, telling him no, just turning another corner.

And then the girl stopped in front of a young woman sitting on a red-and-blue carpet. The woman seemed to be less than twenty years old. She had dark hair, and she looked familiar, like someone he had seen in an old photograph.

This was the image the creatures had showed Lilly when she had asked them about the previous medium. This was the person Marco had thought right away might be Aunt Martha.

But something was missing from the image Lilly had described to him. Marco couldn't remember what it was.

The girl like Lilly was still there. But, oddly, Marco could not see her face, no matter which way she looked.

Marco stopped in front of the woman on the rug. When she looked at him she smiled slowly, knowingly, as if she weren't particularly surprised to see him. But she didn't seem to see the girl like Lilly.

Lilly wasn't saying anything, or thinking anything at him now. He was on his own. And Marco had never been shy. "Are you . . . Aunt Martha?" he asked the woman.

"I am your aunt Martha, though I don't know your name," the woman said, her voice very much like their mother's. She was wearing a long dress the same colors as the carpet, and her dark hair cascaded down her back. "But I know you are my sister Marjorie's son. Funny, I was expecting her daughter. But come and sit down anyway." She patted the carpet.

Marco was sure he didn't have time for a leisurely chat.

But it suddenly struck him: Could Aunt Martha have the answer to what he was looking for?

"I'm Marco," he said.

"Welcome, Marco," she said. "I can feel that you are a kindred spirit. You have been exploring for years, haven't you."

It was not a question. How much else did she know? What did he need to find out from her?

"Were you their medium before?" Marco asked her. "What happened? Why do they need us now, if they had you? And if you're Aunt Martha, how can you be so young?"

"You should know the answer to that last question. Time moves differently for travelers like you and me. And as for being their medium . . ." She shrugged. "Once I learned the ropes, I decided I had better things to do, worlds in many universes to explore. Didn't you find them rather dull . . . and untrustworthy too?"

What was she saying? Yes, the creatures were not terribly fun or exciting. "But what about the danger from the singularity?" Marco burst out.

She lifted her hands, and smiled in a conspiratorial way. "When the singularity goes over the edge, the explosion won't come here," she said lightly. "This universe is safe. That's why I came here. It's a marvelous place." She patted the rug again. "Stay awhile. You'll love it, I promise you."

Part of Marco was horrified. How could she be so selfish, so irresponsible? Didn't she care that the singularity was going to destroy *their* world?

But another part of him was tempted. She was living exactly the kind of life he had always dreamed of, full of adventure, and free from worry and dull responsibilities. And she hadn't aged! She seemed to have the ability to stay young forever.

"And you do too, Marco." She seemed to understand his wondering stare. "It's in your backpack. Take advantage of it. The fact that you got here means you risked your life on their barbaric contraption to win it. So did I."

"You rode the swing? To get a box like mine? A box that controls gravity?"

"Gravity . . . and time. When you decrease gravity with your box, you are speeding up time. When you increase gravity, you are slowing time," she said.

The girl like Lilly moved away.

"Gravity and time are inextricable—except for one major exception." Aunt Martha paused for a moment, her eyes losing focus, giving more importance to the exception.

What was the exception?

Then she became talkative again. "But the exception doesn't pertain to you. With the boxes you and I won on the giant swing we can control our own personal time. We can make time move more quickly, just for ourselves, or, better yet, we can create our own personal slowdowns— time stops for us, and the rest of the world speeds ahead. That way we can stay young as long as we want."

That was exciting all right. But her mention of the word "box" jolted his memory. That's what had been in the image Lilly described, and what was missing now: the box on the rug in front of Aunt Martha.

He remembered what the creatures had just told him, about something called the master box, which had been stolen, and which he had to bring back in order to accomplish their task.

Had Aunt Martha stolen it?

That made sense. Lilly had brought him directly here. Aunt Martha had had a box in the image. And she seemed to be just the kind of reckless person who *would* steal something so important.

He turned and looked after the girl like Lilly. She had stopped at the next stall. But he knew she wouldn't wait for long.

Marco was too rushed to be subtle. "But aren't you worried about what the creatures said?"

"You believe everything they say?" she asked him, with a mocking lilt to her voice. "Stay here and explore. Why do you want to go back *there,* to our boring old world, with the cold and the dreary worries?"

Why, indeed, except to save it? If that was even necessary. "You don't . . . believe what they said about the singularity destroying our world?" he asked her, tempted again.

"Why do you?"

Why did he? he wondered. If he didn't believe that, he would be free, to explore forever in these unimaginably tantalizing places. He felt a weight drop away from him, just as it had when he had first activated his own personal box.

And then the weight sank back down upon him. He believed what the creatures said because Lilly believed. If he did not rush back now with the master box, he would be betraying her utterly. No matter what Aunt Martha said, he could never do that to Lilly. He had to get the master box from her.

But Aunt Martha mustn't know he wanted it. If she knew that, he would have no chance of getting it. He was going to have to steal it from her, as he assumed—hoped—she had stolen it from the creatures. Maybe it was underhanded of him, but he was only doing it to save their own world, which Aunt Martha didn't seem to care about.

The master box seemed to be a *different* box from the ones she was talking about, the boxes they had both won on the giant swing, which they could use to control their gravity and personal time.

"Create our own personal slowdowns," she had said. . . .

"You said . . . we can slow down our own personal time?" he asked her.

"Of course," she answered, casually lifting her hand. "And also speed it up if we like. You already know that. You never would have gotten out of the singularity radius if you hadn't used the box to accelerate time and lessen gravity."

"Yes, but . . . I didn't know about slowing it down. What would that feel like? Look like?"

She laughed. "You're a funny boy. What are you getting at?"

Marco then remembered that he was only twelve, and small. "Could you . . . show me?" he dared to suggest.

"Don't be so silly! There's nothing to show. You just turn into a statue."

"But what does it look like?" Maybe he looked younger. Maybe he could act younger. "Please?" he urged her. "I want to see it *so much*!"

She laughed again, shaking her head. She started to reach behind her, then stopped.

The girl like Lilly was moving away from the next stall. There were people in between them now. Soon he would lose her. He couldn't let that happen.

"Please?" he begged Aunt Martha again.

Aunt Martha sighed and shook her head. "Didn't your mother teach you any—" Then she stopped speaking, her eyes losing focus. She bit her lip. Was she thinking about his mother—her sister? The sister she had run away from and would probably never see again.

Marco stared hard at her, making his eyes wide and innocent.

"You look so much like her," Aunt Martha murmured. She straightened up. She looked around carefully to be sure no one was watching. Then she turned and quickly reached into a dark, curtained alcove behind her. And out of it she took a box. A box exactly like his box, with a knob and a dial. Not the master box, a personal box.

He hoped it was not the only box she had.

She set it down in front of her. "You'll . . . stay with me here awhile, if I show you?" she asked him.

He nodded eagerly.

"Just a small slowdown, since you're so insistent," she said a little irritably. "Please stand guard so no one robs me while I'm gone." She put her hand into the box and turned the knob to the left.

Her hand moved slower, and slower, and slower, and then stopped.

She wasn't breathing now. Her hair drifted in a slight breeze, but aside from that she could have been a lifelike plastic statue. Her eyes were fixed on the spot where he stood.

She could probably see him move, but he couldn't worry

about that. He had to work fast—she said it was just a small slowdown. But he hoped she was frozen deeply enough so that it would take her a while to come out of it.

He darted behind her and peered into the alcove from which she had taken her personal box. It was too dark to see anything inside. Fighting panic, he pulled the curtain aside.

And there was another box. A larger box. It was open at the top. Inside was a kind of propeller, with four oddly shaped curving blades. In the center was a round dial. Gnarled and twisted rootlike things clung to the inside surfaces of the metal box.

He didn't like it. There was something brooding and sinister about it. And it was so big! Could he even carry it? Even if he could, people would surely notice, and take it from him. It was hopeless.

But he had to try. He grabbed a corner of the box and tried to pull it toward him.

As soon as he touched the box, a metal cover rolled across the top, hiding the inside.

He didn't know what it meant, he just knew he had to get it out of here. He looked for an instant at Aunt Martha. Was her hand moving back the other way inside her personal box? It was hard to tell. He started to drag the master box out of the alcove.

He couldn't budge it—it was too heavy.

Aunt Martha's hand was definitely moving now.

He tugged the box harder, grunting. Now it moved a little. But he would never be able to carry this all the way back to the creatures' planet—it was so heavy, and he was running out of time.

But now he had control of time—time and gravity. He could use his personal box to speed up his own time—and lessen the weight of the master box.

He shrugged off his backpack and pulled out his personal box.

Aunt Martha's eyes shifted to follow him. Her upper lip slowly pulled back, exposing her teeth, like the beginning of a snarl.

His hand shaking and sweating, he turned the knob on his personal box to the right, toward the lines that were spaced closer together. Immediately the market square was moving in slow motion, like a movie at the wrong speed. He slipped his personal box back into the backpack. Then quickly, quickly he lifted the master box. He could pick it up easily now. It was so big it was awkward to carry, but he had to try.

The girl like Lilly was drifting slowly past another stall. He glanced back at Aunt Martha. She was speeding up. Was she using her personal box to match his accelerated time?

Marco ran after Lilly. His movements felt so light! He

had finally accomplished something completely on his own, without her help. He had gotten this box, and no one had told him how to do it. He could feel proud about that.

"Get him! He stole my box!" Aunt Martha shrieked behind him. He couldn't help turning back. Two hooded figures were trying to run after him now, pushing through the crowd—but it was as if they were moving through water, they were so much slower.

But Aunt Martha was moving fast, still screaming at him to stop.

The girl emerged from the dark maze into the light again, dappled light, a park of many trees. He could see tall treetops over the horizon. And floating just in front of one of the trees was a hole, a break in space—a wormhole leading back to the singularity radius.

He looked back. Aunt Martha was rushing into the park.

The girl stood facing away from him.

Go now, Marco. No time to lose. If you wait, it will be too late. Her voice was deep and slow now.

But how do I get back?

Hurry! Through the wormhole. Then straight ahead and you'll see—

She was gone, in the middle of a sentence. The girl vanished, and her time-distorted voice, and her directions. Gone. What had happened to Lilly? Had someone hurt her?

Lilly would never leave him voluntarily like this. She was in trouble.

He had to get back to her and find out. And suddenly nothing was more important than that. How long had she been at home, alone with their secret, tormented by Dr. Goldman? How long had he deserted her? He had to get home and help her.

A hand pulled him roughly back by his shoulder. Aunt Martha's quick breath rasped in his ear.

The wormhole was shrinking.

With all his strength he pulled away from her grasp and rushed through, pushing the master box ahead of him.

He was back in the maze of wormholes. But straight ahead, through a ragged opening, he saw something different, a hint of something that might be an end, maybe even an exit from this place. He had to get out of here on his own, back to the creatures' planet.

If he could.

The longer he waited the more impossible it would be. He had seen a glimpse of something clear and solid, something like sky. Was it where Lilly had been directing him? He could only hope it was. And if he didn't get there instantly, it would be lost to him. Forever.

He ran for the ragged hole, forgot to look down, stepped with one foot into a pit, and only barely managed not to tumble into it, to pull out his foot, tripping, and head for the opening.

The opening that was now shrinking.

Another wormhole suddenly spread apart underneath him. He darted around it. The hole he was aiming for was still there but getting smaller. Light flashed on the other side of it.

Another pit blocking his way. It was almost as though the maze were taunting him on purpose, showing him the right way out and then preventing him from reaching it.

He squeezed past the pit and the hole was still there. But was it even big enough for him to get through anymore?

He lunged for it. He pushed the master box through, but the hole closed around his torso. He wiggled, finally kicking at the foamlike edges.

And broke through.

Light raged around him as he fell.

CHAPTER EIGHTEEN

He landed next to the master box, just inside the wall, among the other objects discarded by the singularity. He had made it back to the right universe, he had done the right thing, because of Lilly. But would he ever see those other universes again?

He couldn't sit here thinking about it. He had to get over the wall fast, before the singularity decided to whisk him back up to it again.

It was bright daylight. Night and day were not blinking on and off, as they had been when he left. And he felt amazingly light for being this close to the singularity.

Then he understood. His personal box was still speeding up his own time, and lightening the gravity he felt.

On the other side of the wall, through the arch, he could see the creatures prostrating themselves. But they weren't breathing. They were statues.

Behind him he heard the rumbling of the singularity. It didn't seem appeased at all. He turned to stare at its erupting fury. The creatures would know how to work the master box and, he hoped—after what he had been through—appease it.

But he didn't have to slow down to their speed and gravity this instant. He could make it easier on himself. Without changing his personal box, he plodded up the ramp and climbed into the chair. The creature statues remained immobile. He put the box from Aunt Martha down beside him. The creatures would bear its weight now. He didn't mind that anymore.

And then he took his personal box out of his backpack and moved the dial back to the middle, the normal setting, so that it pointed at the alien symbol.

In an instant the sky became a gray haze of night and day blinking on and off. He felt as if he had been struck by a sledgehammer as gravity slammed him back down into the chair. He had never been so tired in his life. Even with his personal box, he wouldn't have the strength to get back to the village of the creatures on his own.

How much time had gone by? There was no way to tell here, no day and night, and he had no sense of how long he had been inside the singularity.

But in that other universe, on the small planet millions of light-years away, he had briefly been in almost normal time. That's why he had been able to understand Lilly. He hated slowing down again, but he needed to talk to the creatures and give them the master box. And then he would hurry home and find out what had happened to Lilly.

The creatures sensed his presence and got up, looking first at the master box.

The Lord has blessed Lilly—oh, and you too, the creatures told him, as though his part in it was a mere afterthought. But there was awe in their thoughts. *We will be safe now. You have brought back the master box, a real piece of The Lord. We will all be heroes.*

Very slowly, and with great effort, they picked him up. They made no further comment, concentrating on making their tedious way forward, bearing the incredible weight of Marco and his heavy boxes. He removed the dark glass from his head and put it in the chair beside him.

They were moving a lot more sluggishly now than they had on the way here—the trip back would take longer because they were so tired.

Finally, as they gradually progressed away from the

gravity of the singularity, and time began to speed up again, the sun and the moons eventually slowed down. By the time they reached the edge of the plateau there were nights and days. Marco felt himself rising up in the chair as he grew less heavy.

We did it, Marco. We did it. Never forget that. Always remember . . .

Lilly. It should have been a relief to hear from her, after she had disappeared so suddenly on the tiny planet. But there was something in the tone of her thoughts now that felt like a closing, an ending. *Lilly, Lilly, what do you mean? What's happening to you?*

There was no response. Now he was more worried about her than before.

He looked at his watch, for whatever that was worth. It was 3:00, only three and a half hours since they had left the village. If the trip back took another hour (they had already been traveling for half an hour—and the whole trip coming here had taken only one hour), then they would reach the village by 4:00, and he might actually get home by 4:10 after all. But he would still be very late. The watch only measured the time experienced by his own body.

The giant swing had stopped—he was glad that barbaric ritual was over. Crowds of creatures lined both sides of the path as they reached the village. He could feel them cheering, even if they didn't do anything as human as clapping their pincers.

Lilly has saved us! Lilly has saved us! they were silently crying out.

What about me? Marco could not keep himself from mentally shouting back at them. *I went there. I was the one who actually faced The Unknowable and went inside it.*

Oh, yes! Marco too, Marco too is our savior, they replied, and he could feel the politeness in their emotion. It was Lilly they were really cheering for, only grudgingly willing to admit that Marco had done anything at all. He couldn't help feeling irritated again.

Yes, yes, you are very brave, Marco. We are beginning to understand. You and Lilly together were the medium.

That was a little better.

This master box I got on the other world. Is this what I need to go everyplace there is to go? he asked them.

Oh, no, you never understand! It is the box you won here on the giant swing that enables you to negotiate the gravity of The Lord and go to all the worlds. You beat gravity on the swing, and so now you can control gravity within The Lord. The master box you brought back from the other world belongs here. It is a piece of The Lord, and shares its properties. It tells us what The Lord wants. It told us to make the tunnel to your world. The Lord meant the master box to be here. Now that we have it back, the world will soon be in balance again. The one who stole it did not understand. You will give it to us now.

It was not a request, it was a command. But he didn't mind handing it to the group of creatures clustered around him, who took it reverently. He still had his own personal box, which would slow *him* down, and keep him young. And with it he could now go everywhere there was to go. What else did he need?

The creatures carried the master box away, around a building, to some secret place.

And in a moment, those in the square all looked up at the sky. Marco looked too. He gasped—and he felt the creatures gasping.

The singularity had changed. It was still spinning. But the violence of light around it had almost completely stopped. It was not painful to look at anymore, no longer an object of dread. Now the sight of it gave him a feeling of peace, even safety. It was like a bright spinning star, with occasional ripples and arcs of lightning branching out of it.

Why had it changed? Because he had gotten the master box from Aunt Martha?

Not just him. Lilly too. Together they had accomplished this monumental task.

Now we must celebrate! We must feast!

They set him down in the town square, beside the motionless giant swing. The first thing he did was to bow to and thank his bearers, who bowed back. Then he looked for the cardboard box that showed him the way to the basement. It was still just where he had left it. They had said they understood about it, and clearly they did—it had been there for many of their days.

He checked his watch. It was 4:03. *I don't have time to celebrate very long,* he told them. *I have to be back soon— and the earlier the better.* But he figured if he stayed a few minutes longer it would only be one more day back at home, and that couldn't make much difference now. And he would enjoy being celebrated.

Oh, yes, yes, we know you think you have to get back so soon. But still, let us honor you. We will keep the ceremony as short as possible. The Lord will like it.

Once Marco would have thought that the singularity didn't care what they did, that it wasn't even capable of emotions. But now he had seen it change; it had calmed down. Maybe there was something to what they believed.

So he sat there feeling proud as they all bowed to him and chanted again in some language he didn't understand—it was probably the same language his bearers had prayed in.

Tired as he was, he actually felt comfortable in this gravity now, which had been so difficult at first. It was *nothing* compared to the gravity near the singularity. He must have grown a lot stronger. At home he would probably feel almost weightless, once he wasn't so exhausted.

And now he was growing more and more impatient to get back. It was almost 4:20. The creatures just kept on praying, and some of them were now doing a kind of ritual dance around him, wearing funny pieces of metal on their heads. How long was this going to go on? What would happen if he just left? He kept surreptitiously looking at his watch, feeling it would be impolite if they noticed. But, after all, they couldn't see.

The dancing stopped. *Yes, we know you are in a hurry to get back. So we have completed only the short form of the ritual. Perhaps it will be enough. You can go back now.*

He climbed out of the chair, carrying his personal box. He knew it was going to be difficult at home, and there were parts of it that he was dreading, such as dealing with his parents. But his need to get back to Lilly was stronger than any of it.

Well, er, good-bye, he thought at them, backing toward the cardboard box.

They all bowed to him at once. *Thank you, Marco. We will see you again soon.*

What did that mean? He didn't wait to ask. He turned and put his personal box into the cardboard box, then pushed it up into the tunnel.

His heart swelled with happiness. He was going home to Lilly at last.

CHAPTER ✦NINETEEN

Lilly was not waiting to meet him, as he had imagined.

The basement was dark; he had to turn on the light. He felt a sinking disappointment that Lilly wasn't there. But that was unrealistic. She couldn't stay in the basement all the time. He'd see her as soon as he went upstairs.

The root cellar looked pretty much the same. How much time had gone by? His heart thudded with anticipation, and apprehension too.

He heard a baby crying. It had been a long time since a baby had cried in this house. Who was visiting?

He would leave his personal box down here for the moment, until the initial confrontation was over. He knew it would not be safe, with Ruth and his parents in the house. Perhaps he could keep his box in the attic room at Nat's, if the bag he had left there was still safe.

He started up the stairs. And in fact he did feel like he was floating, even as tired as he was. Climbing the stairs was as effortless as walking downhill. It was a kind of dreamlike sensation.

The baby was still screaming, and he heard conversation. But not real conversation. What was going on?

He had no idea what he was going to be faced with, or how many weeks he had been gone. And so he didn't make a plan. He just followed the sounds of the crying baby into the living room.

An unattractive overweight woman sat in a big ugly recliner chair, puffing on a cigarette and watching a strangely futuristic TV. She halfheartedly rocked the cradle next to her, her eyes fixed on the television, ignoring the crying baby. She was so absorbed—and Marco walked so lightly—that she didn't even look up when he stepped into the doorway.

He was scared. Who was this woman? Who was the baby? They didn't seem like visitors, they looked like they were living here. And yet, except for the TV and the recliner, the rest of the furniture was the same as before—though to his eyes now it seemed shabbier. So where were Lilly, and his parents, and Ruth?

He walked into the room, feeling uncharacteristically shy. "Er, excuse me," he said.

The woman jerked in her seat, then turned and looked at him, startled. Her expression was hostile. "Where did you come from?" she demanded.

Normally Marco was confident, not shy. But this situation was more unnerving than almost anything he had faced so far. "I'm . . . Marco," he said. "I live here, with my parents and my two sisters. Where are they?"

The woman frowned. Then she thought of something and turned and looked at a picture on the mantel, still not getting up. When she looked back at Marco, her mouth dropped open. "Lilly said . . . this might happen," she murmured, as if reassuring herself that it was possible. "She said it right before she—" Then she clamped her mouth shut, suddenly registering that Marco was listening.

"Right before she what?" Marco asked, now too curious to be shy.

The woman didn't answer. She turned and looked at the picture on the mantel again, then back at Marco, her face pale. Who was she, anyway?

"Where's my family?" Marco said more forcefully.

"You have to prove who you are," the woman said, forgetting to rock the baby, who was crying louder than ever.

Now Marco was getting a little riled. Why was this person making demands on him? "But this is our house. Why do I have to prove anything?"

"Because I say so," the woman said, stabbing out her cigarette with finality. "Say something to prove who you are."

He didn't like feeling at a disadvantage with this person, but he had no choice—she was clearly in control here. "I'm Marco, I'm twelve, I live here with my parents and my two sisters—Lilly, who's eleven, and Ruth, who's seven. Our mother works at home and our father works—"

"Where did you come from just now?" the woman wanted to know.

He couldn't think of a lie. "From the basement," he said lamely. "I came up from the basement."

Oddly, that seemed to satisfy her. "He looks exactly the same," she murmured to herself again, staring at him. "And she said he would come from the basement. . . ."

"Who said?" Marco asked her.

"Lilly. My older sister, Lilly," she said flatly.

"Your older sister, Lilly?" Marco repeated, baffled. Okay, she had a sister named Lilly. But what did that have to do with proving who *he* was? She was still watching him. "So . . . you have a sister named Lilly too?" he said, feeling stupid.

"The *same* sister," the woman said slowly. "I'm Ruth."

Marco still didn't understand. "That's a coincidence," he said, shrugging slightly. "Another Lilly and Ruth."

Now the woman's fat features almost looked concerned. "You have no idea how long you've been gone?" she asked him in a hushed voice.

"You believe who I am now? You know how long I've been away?" he asked, moving eagerly toward her.

"Twenty-three years, Marco," she said. And her expression changed from that hint of concern to something a lot more like gloating. "You've been away twenty-three years. You're still twelve and I'm thirty—Lilly said it would be like that. And Lilly . . ." Her voice faded.

Marco stopped moving. Was it possible? His mind raced back to the slow world, the singularity, how the slow world had speeded up so much when they were on the plateau, meaning this world had been rocketing ahead many times more.

Twenty-three years. He had never imagined that. It was hard to imagine even now, and he felt numb. But when he looked at it scientifically it seemed possible, even likely.

That meant Lilly was thirty-four. The woman—Ruth!—had mentioned Lilly's name several times, but had never said anything about her. "Where's Lilly?" Marco said, moving closer, fixing her with his eyes. "Where is she? I have to see her right now!"

The woman looked down. She pulled at her lower lip with one hand, then quickly put another cigarette in her mouth and lit it, still not looking at him.

"Where's Lilly?" Marco demanded, feeling scared.

"The accident was . . . four months ago," Ruth said, staring at her cigarette. "Just after her daughter, Annie, was born. Lilly knew something was going to happen—she always did. I don't think she knew exactly what it was, but she knew she didn't have much time. She told me you might be coming back and to take good care of Annie. . . ."

"What happened!" Marco shouted, next to her now, his hands gripping the arm of her chair, his face on a level with hers.

"A car accident, a car accident, okay!" Ruth shouted back, breathing heavily. "She and Carl and Mom and Dad. A head-on collision, no survivors. I'm Annie's legal guardian now."

The baby was still screaming.

"No," Marco said softly. What she was saying wasn't possible. He had been numb before; he felt frozen now. "No. She's . . . you must be . . . I just heard from her a little while ago, only a few minutes . . ." But of course what he had heard from Lilly on the plateau on the way back from the singularity was *not* just a few minutes ago, it could easily have been four months, in this world's time.

He sank down weakly into another chair in front of the

TV, which was running some kind of game show. The baby was still crying. He didn't hear any of it.

"Why would I lie?" Ruth was saying. "Like I said, Lilly knew something was going to happen. Not exactly what or when, or they wouldn't have gone. But she told me to keep an eye out for you. And she said when I saw you, I should tell you, 'Annie's hairs will work.' Whatever that means. Typical of her."

"Annie's hairs will work," Marco mumbled, feeling the tears now. It was that, more than anything else Ruth said, that brought it home to him. Because Lilly would have thought of that. She knew she wouldn't be here when he came back. So she had to be sure he knew how to get through the tunnel so that he could still travel, so that he could go everywhere there was to go.

He put his hands over his eyes and bent forward in the chair, tears streaming from his eyes, trying to gulp back his sobs in front of this Ruth creature. "Can I . . . can I go up to my room now?" he managed to say. He had to be alone.

"It's the same as it always was. Only . . . I'm not sure how much I want you around," Ruth said.

He glanced sharply at her. Her face was blurred through his tears. But he almost thought he saw a kind of fear in her eyes. And why shouldn't she be afraid? They had always made sure she hated the basement, and now he had come up from it, unchanged after twenty-three years. He must seem like a ghost to her.

"I'll be going up now," Marco said. "Don't worry, I won't stay around here much. But I'll come back—to check on Annie."

Marco got up and went over to the baby. Marco was uncomfortable around babies, but this one was so special! He reached out and gently touched her tiny hand. Miraculously, she stopped crying. "She's beautiful," he whispered. "Like her mother."

"Don't!" Ruth said, putting her hand to her mouth.

"Don't what?" Marco asked her, touching Annie's hand again.

"You can baby-sit occasionally, but I just . . . don't want you getting too attached to the baby, that's all," Ruth said, blowing out smoke before crushing her cigarette.

Ruth wanted to protect Lilly's child from him? Marco would have to find out more. "It's not good to smoke cigarettes around babies," he said, for the moment.

Ruth's expression changed to a glower. "If you *do* want to baby-sit, you better—"

Marco had to play it cool. "Whatever you say. See you later," he said.

Up in his room, he kneeled on the floor and rocked with sobs for a long, long time, thinking of his parents and of

Lilly, of all the times with her, and all the times he had left her alone. If only he could have some of that time back! He knew he would grieve for her for the rest of his life.

He wanted to get away from this sad place, and now he really could go everywhere there was to go. But even that was a mixed blessing. He might have beaten gravity, but time had beaten him in the end.

He would always come back, to make sure Annie was treated well and had everything she needed. He would give Lilly's child the love that Ruth couldn't give.

He entered the tunnel the next day, with a piece of one of Annie's hairs. The creatures did not seem surprised to see him. He greeted them politely, and then turned the dial on his personal box—the direction that speeded him up and lessened gravity. The world stopped. He hurried past the statue creatures all the way to the plateau, and over the wall, and back inside the singularity radius again. The wormholes would take him everywhere there was to go.

And Marco traveled, millions and millions of light-years. To dark, barren rocky worlds, to worlds of jungles, to worlds of endless partying cities, to worlds where time went faster, and where time went slower. To find the wormhole that led home, he followed the sound of Annie crying in his head.

When he felt meditative, he went back to the turret room at Nat's house, and sat outside, safely invisible, and slowed himself down, and watched the world speed by.

He would have loved to see the spherical city again, but he was afraid to go back. What would Aunt Martha do if she ever found him? His fear of her was also why he never stayed at home very long—she had grown up in that house too and could easily find him there.

He looked over his shoulder a lot.

He knew the creatures would be more careful of the master box this time. The most important thing they told him was that Annie was the next medium.

He found a cozy little world, which he hoped was safer from Aunt Martha than Earth was, where he could stay and rest when he was tired from traveling. He made a home there.

He came back often, to be with Annie.

And Annie grew.